Watch Over Me
Navajo Code Talkers Book 2
Eileen Charbonneau

Print ISBNs
Barnes & Noble 9780228629993
Amazon Print 9781773623887
Ingram Spark 9781773623863

Copyright 2017 Eileen Charbonneau
Cover by Michelle Lee

All rights reserved. Without limiting the rights under copyright reserved above, no part of this publication may be reproduced, stored in or introduced into a retrieval system, or transmitted, in any form, or by any means (electronic, mechanical, photocopying, recording, or otherwise) without prior written permission of both the copyright owner and the publisher of this book.

Dedication

For New York, City of Dreams

Table of Contents

Chapter 1 6
Chapter 2 26
Chapter 3 38
Chapter 4 48
Chapter 5 55
Chapter 6 68
Chapter 7 81
Chapter 8 96
Chapter 9 103
Chapter 10 115
Chapter 11 127
Chapter 12 137
Chapter 13 146
Chapter 14 162
Chapter 15 169
Chapter 16 177
Chapter 17 186
Chapter 18 195
Chapter 19 201
Chapter 20 204
Chapter 21 213
Chapter 22 219
Chapter 23 226

Chapter 1

July, 1942
***Spenser International Headquarters,
Midtown Manhattan***

Kitty could only see the back of the man sitting beyond the glass wall. His fedora rested on his knees. The late morning sunlight came through the office waiting room's vaulted, bronze-clad windows, highlighting sharp shoulders beneath his elegant linen suit. His hands were shaking.

"What's wrong with him?" she asked.

Jack Spenser sighed. "He had a hard time of it in Spain, Kitty. But he's all right now."

Her boss sounded like he was trying to convince them both. He pressed a wad of bills into her hand. "Listen. This one is the quiet type, and a gentleman. He's been reading up on New York from an old guidebook. A few of the sights, a meal, then tuck him in early at the St. Pierre. That's all."

"I'm not your girl for this, Jack."

He exhaled. Kitty figured that his patience with her was running out. "Well, he asked for you, so I owed him a try, but I suppose Gloria would be willing."

Gloria was a clinging vine, had a Betty Boop voice and chattered constantly. Kitty shook her head. "Aw, don't scare the poor guy back to Spain."

Jack grinned. "You won't regret it," he promised.

She was already regretting it.

He opened the door. "Kitty Charente, meet Luke Kayenta."

The man stood. He was a generation younger than Jack Spenser. Early twenties, she guessed, maybe even younger than Kitty's twenty-four years. He was much taller than her Philippe, who had fit into his cockpit with a panther's grace. Stop thinking of Philippe, she admonished herself. Start smiling.

"Welcome to New York, Mr. Kayenta," she said.

"Yes. Thank you, Ma'am."

Dark. Exotic, almond-shaped eyes, poker straight black hair, cut short. Kitty didn't usually get the young ones, even when they caught sight of her legs under her switchboard and asked for her. And if he'd asked for her, why didn't she remember seeing him before now?

He flashed a pained look at Jack.

Wow. Very shy. Kitty could not picture any exclusive shopkeepers buying Spenser International's perfumes from Luke Kayenta, despite his nice suit, his gold watch chain. But then, he wasn't the first Spenser International salesman who'd struck her that way.

"Enjoy our city. Get out of here, the both of you," Jack ordered.

They made it though the offices and showrooms, down the elevator, and through the marble and bronze lobby, with only a bit of him staring at the frozen fountain motifs and inlaid stars on the barrel vaulted ceiling. But Kitty had to grab for the crook of her charge's arm as they hit the street or the noon crowd would have swallowed him. She reigned him in against the building's limestone

"Want to get a nosh first?"

Something brightened in his face. "Nosh," he sounded out slowly. "This means a small meal, yes?"

"That's right."

"It is a Yiddish word. You are one of the Jewish people, then?"

"Naw, just a New Yorker. We pick up words from each other, you know?"

He shook his head. "Sorry?"

Each word came out of him slowly, precisely. He didn't grow up speaking English, she guessed. Kitty couldn't place his accent, or cadence, or his unusual nasal drawl. He winced at the blare of a taxi's horn. What a rube.

"Hey, you want to eat or not?"

"Not. No, Ma'am."

"Would you stop calling me 'Ma'am.' I'm not your grandmother."

"No."

Damn. Shy to begin with, and she'd cut him down to one syllable already. She tried again, slowly. "Jack says you've been reading up on our city. Any ideas for a first stop?"

"Yes."

"Where?"

"The Empire State Building. Where King Kong fought off the aeroplanes."

Aeroplanes? This was going to be a long day. "That's close by. We can walk." She grabbed his hand. Strong, but soft and supple. And not shaking, now.

He allowed Kitty to pull him into the street's flow of busy New Yorkers, but a few blocks later, as they stood on the corner of 33rd and Fifth Avenue, Luke Kayenta quietly insisted he had to climb on foot to the top of the world's tallest building.

"Do you know how many stories that is?" she demanded.

"One hundred and two. It is the top place of Manhattan Island--one thousand two hundred and fifty feet high. Then, a tower, yes?"

"So what's the matter with elevators?"

"Nothing. I like to climb."

Country rube, afraid of elevators was more likely, Kitty thought, but managed not to snort. "Look, Mr. Kayenta," she directed his attention down her leg. "These are new shoes. And get a load of the heels, will you?" She turned, showing her Kerrybrook cherry pumps with their baby doll round toes and open lattice work. Shoes. Her indulgence, even in wartime.

His sharp intake of breath whistled. But he wasn't smiling, the way other men did when they looked her over. Did he ever smile?

"My shoes are new, too," he drawled out softly. "Maybe we should take them off?"

"What? My stockings would shred to pieces!" They were nylon stockings that Philippe had supplied, courtesy of Royal Air Force contraband.

That blank look showed up again on his face. Exasperated, Kitty reached down to her calf, took a piece of clinging nylon between her fingers, and snapped. "Stockings! See?"

He winced, swallowing. He was mortified at the sight of a little leg. Holy Hannah, Kitty thought, Gloria would have eaten this one alive.

"Stockings off too," he proposed. "Bare feet. For both of us." He eyed her shoulder bag. "I will carry your gear. I will carry you, if you get tired, Mrs. Charente."

Something bubbled up in Kitty at the absurdity of their conversation. A laugh. Hollow, her devastation bleeding out of it, but a laugh.

"Well, if we'll be showing our feet to each other, you'd better call me Kitty," she told him.

"Is this a custom?"

Aeroplanes. Customs. "You're not from around here, are you?"

One of his brows arched, disappearing in the shadow cast by his hat's wide rim. "You can tell?" Well. He understood teasing, at least.

So, once inside the lobby, Kitty ignored the perfectly serviceable banks of elevators and through the stairwell door. Luke Kayenta slipped his feet out of his shoes, and tugged his socks off too. While he was busy tying the laces together, she stood behind him on the landing. "Eyes front," she admonished, as she kicked off her shoes unhitched her garter belt and removed her stockings, stuffing both into her pocketbook. He stayed stock still until she touched his shoulder. True to his word, he took her shoes and placed them under his arm.

"If you are to be called Kitty, I should be Luke, then, maybe?"

"Deal."

"Deal?"

"Agreement?"

"Ah, yes."

"Now, listen," she connived, for the sake of her feet, "You don't seem like an inside kind of fella to me." His deep tan gave that away easily enough. "We don't have to climb all the way up the tower, do we? The deck on the eighty-sixth floor has the best views, and an outside walkway."

His eyes brightened. "Yes. Might we go to that place, please?"

"You're the boss."

He frowned. "No. Your guest."

"And the Spenser International guest is always right," she pronounced, clipping sixteen floors off their climb.

* * *

How was he to find any spirit guidance here, in this loud place, full of beings flitting about like hummingbirds, Luke wondered. The letter now placed against his heart had survived the way he had, hidden. He must stay hidden among them. But remember. Remember who he was, even while climbing endless steps in a gray, airless place, the Empire State Building's stairwell, a place like his cell.

There had been no light, no air there either.

The scent of his flesh burning returned from where he thought he had banished them—his dreamtime. His heart raced. Stop. Not here. Not before this woman. Promises. He had promises to keep. And miles to go, he remembered the words from the poet, the one whose spare, graceful stanzas reminded him of the songs of his people. He recited the poem in his mind, to calm it, to slow down the beat of his heart.

Miles to go, before I sleep.

There. Travel those miles. Westward. Return home, where his superiors would not allow him to go. Not yet. But he could fly this way, in his mind. Home. Where the women would smile, his mother proud of his new rank, his standing in the world of the belegaanas. His grandmother would have a Blessing Way done, to ask the Holy People to watch over him. But first, an Enemy Way ceremony. He needed that so badly.

"Thrill's not gone yet, huh?" Kitty Charente asked him, panting, as she collapsed on the landing of the stairs marked with the number twenty-nine. Her exhaustion slowed down her running together speech enough for Luke to finally understand her easily. "Hey, don't they have nice, tall buildings enough in Spain for you?"

Luke felt his mother's frown. Caught up in his thoughts of his own troubles, he had not noticed a woman's weariness. He pushed back his hat and squatted down beside her.

"No tall buildings. When in Spain, I lived in the mountains."

Eyes as dark as his own women's challenged him. "You didn't sell perfume in the mountains."

"No."

His shoes, their laces tied together and carried over his shoulder, clunked softly against hers, tucked under his arm, both pairs scented with new leather. Luke sat beside the airman's wife.

"This stairway climbing was not such a good idea, maybe. I'm sorry, Kitty."

She closed her eyes. Was she out of patience with him? He approached closer, closer than he would have with a woman at home if she had looked so displeased.

"We should find an elevator to take us the rest of the way, maybe?" he tried.

"But, I thought, I mean..."

"What did you think?"

She looked down at her toes, shining, their nails painted red, like her mouth, like the hat framing her head, her lustrous hair. Had this woman who was beyond beautiful think he was afraid of elevators?

"Never mind," she snapped. It sounded like, "nevermind." Her words were running together again. "Comeon," became "Come on."

Having to break up her fast talk in his mind made Luke feel thick, slow.

Kitty opened the door with the number of the floor marked on it, and guided him through.

On the other side of that door, the world changed. The space was higher, brighter, bigger, gleaming with shining metalwork. No longer like his cell, this was again the big, bold front-face world of this city: full of bronze and marble and electric lights of enchantment.

They stood in this world barefooted, a fact even the bustling hummingbird people now swarming around them noticed. And pointed at them, rudely. Foolish. They looked foolish here, without their shoes on.

The airman's wife tugged at his sleeve. Wry, exasperated amusement joined the deep sadness living in Kitty Charente's eyes. This was good. Luke knew that look, many women at home used it. On him, on most of the men. He surrendered her shoes to her. Red shoes, the color of his grandmother's ceremonial skirt.

* * *

Once out on the observation deck, Kitty watched Jack's stray salesman transform out of his shyness. Like a kid, he couldn't get enough of the high summer clouds, the canyons of skyscrapers below them. Even the jostling crowd of fellow sightseers didn't seem to bother him up here.

He leaned over the ledge. "That one. It looks like a toy."

"There are lots of toys in there. That's Macy's, the world's largest store."

"How large?"

Kitty was ready. "Two million square feet." Men loved numbers, so she'd memorized enough of them to impress Jack's strays.

"I can't imagine needing so many things," he said.

"No? It must have been tough to sell perfume with that attitude."

He shrugged before walking to the south facing side of the building.

"That one, Kitty." He thrust out his chin, instead of pointing. Philippe pointed all the time. At maps, at his fancy air-route globe, at the sun going down over the skyline. "Do you know the name of that place?" Luke asked her. "The one like an arrowhead?"

"The Flatiron building?"

"Flat iron, yes. Also arrowhead, I think. It pleases me."

"It's very old. One of the first skyscrapers. That used to be the windiest corner of Manhattan, twenty-third and fifth. The cops— policemen, they used to shoo away the swells who stood by the Flatiron, hoping for a peek at the ankles of girls passing by, way back before the last war."

"What are swells?"

"Fellas. You know. Looking for a good time."

"From seeing ankles?"

"Well, it was all they could hope for back then, when women were more covered."

"Oh. But, Kitty, this word... "

"Never mind. If you have to explain 'em, they ain't funny."

"No. I'm sure it is funny. My understanding is not complete enough."

"Forget it. Enjoy the view."

He talked so little. Still, that earnest drawl was making her even more irritated than his silence. Luke Kayenta was young, lonely, recovering from whatever his "rough time of it" was. And red-blooded male, for all his courtly behavior. She knew that from the way he watched the sway of her skirt, and grinned at the laugh of the blond who walked about the deck with a sailor on each arm. Maybe Jack should have gotten Gloria to show him around, then take him to her place, to fuck his loneliness away, Kitty thought. She was not good at any of this hospitality-to-the-salesmen nonsense any more.

"See the speck to the right?" she demanded, like the worst-tempered tour guide, even in New York. "See it? In the harbor?"

"Yes."

"That's the Statue of Liberty."

He nodded. "A gift from France. She is made of copper. American schoolchildren paid for the base."

She dropped a nickel in the big sightseeing binoculars. "Go on. Look closer."

Kitty felt his rapt attention as he molded his tall frame to the machine.

"She's my mother's rival, that French hussy," she said impulsively rattling into the family story her nephews and niece always asked for. Maybe if she imagined him a kid, she could be nicer to him.

He took his wind-blown head out of the view, and gave her his full attention. When had he taken off his hat? He wore no dressing in his dense black hair, so although neatly cut, it looked wild.

"Tell me of this," he said softly.

The lunch hour crowd had left the Observation Deck. They were alone. Kitty stepped back. There was too much of him, that big hand pulling the poker straight hair back from his forehead.

Kitty faced the Hudson again. "My father came here from Croatia, a place in Eastern Europe which isn't even a country any more since Austria gobbled it up, before Hitler gobbled up Austria. They even changed Pop's name, which was Barichievich, to Berry when they processed him at Ellis Island. Anyway, the Statue of Liberty was the first thing he saw here, in America, when he was like the poem, you know: poor, huddled, yearning to be free?"

"I don't know it. Tell me this poem."

"Really?"

"Really."

"Well. Pop had all of us kids memorize Miss Liberty's words by the time we were five." Kitty cleared her throat awkwardly.

> "Keep, ancient lands, your storied pomp!"
> Cries she with silent lips.
> "Give me your tired, your poor,
> Your huddled masses yearning to breathe free,
> The wretched refuse of your teeming shore.
> Send these, the homeless, tempest-tost to me.
> I lift my lamp beside the golden door."

She wasn't looking at him. But she could feel the intensity of Luke Kayenta's eyes. "Pop," she heard herself babble on, "he says Mama was the second American beauty he saw, after Lady Liberty. She was flipping pancakes in the window of Childs Restaurant. Mama was not too tall for him like the statue was, so he married her."

Luke Kayenta smiled. He could smile, then. His teeth were straight and white.

"A good story," he said. "You honor me with it."

"You... talk like an old book."

"Do I?"

He found Central Park next. "Are they hiding beneath the trees?" he asked as Kitty pointed out the Sheep Meadow.

"Are who hiding?"

"The sheep."

"There are no sheep down there."

"But the book said... "

"Your guidebook's out of date. They got shipped out to Brooklyn in thirty-four."

"Why?"

"To make room for Tavern on the Green, see?"

But his attention stayed on the meadow.

"It is a good place for sheep," he declared stubbornly.

"Was, until the Depression. Homeless people started living in the park then, and stealing the sheep."

"For the wool?"

"To eat."

"Oh, of course."

Luke Kayenta was the most peculiar of Jack Spenser's men yet, Kitty decided. But at least he didn't have the over-educated self-importance of most of them.

He looked up toward the Empire State Building's remaining floors and its pinnacle tower, where King Kong had swatted at those fighter planes.

"Thank you for bringing me to this place, Kitty," he said.

"You're welcome." Was that her voice, so soft? Where was her gum? She needed gum to crack, though Jack would have taken a dim view of it. Gloria was the gum chewer, the good-time girl. Kitty was for the shy ones, the faithful husbands, the ones who wanted company, not temptation.

"How many times did you see the picture?" she asked.

"Picture?"

"The movie, you know. King Kong?"

"Oh. I never saw it."

"But, how—?"

"My friend, he saw it. He loved telling me the story. We planned to come here together."

"And, he isn't going to make it, is he?"

He looked out over the Hudson. "No."

She knew the final sound of that "no." But how had a perfume salesman found death in neutral Spain?

"It was a good story too, King Kong," Luke continued. "He told it to me many times. How beauty killed the beast. We didn't understand that part. It seemed to us the man who brought the animal here to New York City was a coward, blaming the woman. She screamed well, my friend said. She honored her anger, her grief." He winced. "I'm sorry. Sometimes I talk too much."

Not too much. He was too close. Yes, she had the best legs in a choice stable of secretaries and switchboard operators at Spenser International, but why had this sad-eyed man really asked Jack for her company?

"Kitty. Please sit here. Wait for me. I'll be back."

He led her to a bench, then soundlessly disappeared around the corner.

A high wind tugged at her skirt. What was he up to? What if he'd promised his friend to do something stupid, like climb the tower as King Kong had? Men were always doing stupid things like climbing steeples, sitting on flagpoles, flying high-risk missions over France for the damned RAF. Luke Kayenta wouldn't do something stupid, would he?

Kitty tried to sit still. But she was in charge of him, wasn't she? What was in his eyes? Death? Did he want to die? It's what she had wanted, after Philippe. The memory of it seared through her, burning wider the hole living in her gut. Sometimes she wondered if it had killed the baby, her desire. The doctor at Saint Vincent's said to put her mind away from there, and concentrate on her own healing.

She had tried. But the trying was so hard. For a little while she'd had them both. And now, she had only the hole. "I'll be back." Philippe had made the same promise, on the last day she ever saw him, held him, made love. Lying bastard.

Kitty rammed herself into the edge of the bench, yanked out her compact with hands shaking worse than Luke Kayenta's had. She pulled out her handkerchief, cleared off the smudge of lipstick on the shining surface. Then she cocked the mirror to peer around the corner behind her.

He was there, his feet still in his shoes, his body still on the observation deck.

She breathed again.

* * *

The airman's wife was watching him. Luke didn't want to frighten her, but he had his duty. He sang the words softly.

Ya-Cith-Kah, Ghin-bi-shai;
Un-deen-tah, Ghin-bi-shai.

High in the clouds, the eagle flies;
With magic wings, the eagle flies

The pneumonia had left his singing voice sounding like a rusted wagon wheel. The one who was not here, his was a fine voice, full of power and laughter. It had sustained Luke through the dark time in Spain, his clan brother's chanting.

Luke felt alone, here at the top of this place of canyons, so different from those at home. Alone, even with this woman he had been dreaming about for so long it seemed like a part of his being, like the power home held over him, or his fascination for the twists and turns of language. He was a burden to her, he knew, a burden she did not like at all. Would she care for him even less once he'd kept his promise to the airman? What would that do to him? Where would he put that black sorrow? Always Luke had his clan brother with whom to talk over such things. He wanted to have that one beside him. Why was he not here?

A disrespectful question. He'd been living among the belegaanas too long.

The wind answered, whistling, reminding him to continue the ceremony.

Luke reached into his pocket, behind the airman's letter, for the sheepskin pouch. He drew it out, took a pinch of corn pollen between his fingers. He sang as he spread grains toward the summer sky. The wind picked them up. A good sign, he judged, though he was not very experienced at this.

He'd been one of those children the elders had chosen long ago, because he listened well. But he had stopped thinking about becoming a singer. Could he ever find that deep-listening child inside himself again? Could he remember the songs he'd learned before the boarding school's harsh Christianity, the college's skepticism, and now, the world gone mad?

Luke faced the place that had given him joy, Central Park, where sheep had once roamed, and released a few more grains. He turned toward the south of this island, where the arrow-shaped building was, and did the same, singing softly. He repeated the ceremony out over each river--the one the belegaanas called East and the one they called the Hudson. He wished he knew the rivers' true names, the names the original people had given to them.

Liberty was the woman in the harbor's name. He now saw her as Kitty Charente's stepmother, her father's first love. Luke thanked Hosteen Liberty for her welcome. His ancestors had been immigrants, too, among the older people, the Hopi and Zuni. The song of the morning dove for Lady Liberty's daughter came into him, so he sang it out:

Yoo-woo-o!
Sh kay-la chee!

Oh look!
I have red shoes!

Luke sprinkled the remaining grains of his offering on his own head as he finished with a song to the birds.
Ee-yaa, Ee-yaa, ah-nin-ne-aye
Up, up, I fly away

Then, he waited. For the birds to answer.

※ ※ ※

After all the strange things she'd witnessed through her mirror, Kitty watched Luke Kayenta's long arms stretch out, as if he was about to take a package. His eyes closed. He didn't make a sound for a long time.

When he opened his eyes again he looked disappointed, as if the package hadn't come.

He then caught the glint of sun reflected in her compact's mirror, she was sure. He slowly, carefully, returned the small stringed bag back inside his shirt, and buttoned it. He replaced the hat to his head. Kitty yanked out her lipstick and did a quick touch up, embarrassed by her spying.

Before she was even finished, he stood above her.

"Thank you," he said quietly.

He looked different: burnished with wildness, but somehow calmer too. Hungry eyes. Plain, for-food hungry. She understood that.

"You need to eat," she told him in her mother's brook-no-argument voice.

"Yes," he agreed, reaching out his hand for hers like an exhausted child.

Kitty felt the soft, leftover grains between the pads of their fingers as they walked toward the elevators. She stopped. Oh, God, she thought, do Spanish people cremate their dead? Was his friend in that pouch?

"Corn," he said quietly. "Corn pollen, that's all. You don't have to be afraid of me, Kitty."

"Afraid?" she snapped. "Who do you think you're talking to? Who's afraid?"

"Hey ya."

The soft call came from the man getting off the elevator, ending their confrontation. As deeply tanned as Luke, he wore an unbuttoned vest over rolled up shirt sleeves. A tweed cap covered his head. He was loaded with the tackling and equipment of his profession— window washer in the world's tallest building.

"Looking for this?" the man asked.

Luke accepted a black and white feather from him. "Ya'eeh te'h," he said.

"Sorry." The window washer shrugged, making his equipment clank together. "I don't talk your talk, brother. I don't even talk my own. Off the res two generations now. I'm a city boy."

Luke nodded. "I am Dinè," he said.

"Kanien'Kahake," the window washer answered, grinning. "Mohawk. We like high places."

Luke placed his hand on the small of Kitty's back, steering her to take the window washer's place in the elevator. He stepped in beside her. The doors closed.

"That wasn't Spanish," she said.

"No."

"But, you do speak Spanish?"

"Si."

Luke Kayenta placed the feather carefully into the breast pocket of his elegant suit. He was very agreeable for someone who was hiding so much, Kitty decided.

Chapter 2

The grand old Hotel Westminster was now frayed around the edges, under basic-only wartime repairs. But the whiskey in its Manhattan was still potent. Kitty finished the cocktail and watched Luke Kayenta demolish the last of a bluefish so big its tail dipped over the edge of the plate. The man ate like he was going to the Chair.

Head waitress Alice Weiss sailed through from the kitchen with yet more leftovers. "Regulars didn't care much for the succotash, we've got extra. Want some, handsome?"

Luke blinked. "Sure. Yes, Ma'am, Miss, ... Alice. Thank you."

She landed the steaming bowl dead on beside the last hunk of his corn bread, grinning. "You, Kitty?"

"No thanks, Alice."

The waitress shifted her slim form's weight to her left side. "Lunch crowd got all of Hank's Boston cream pie. Bread pudding's crusty. Can't recommend a thing for dessert. Say, you can take Luke to Rumplemeyer's, after a nice walk, maybe in the park?"

Alice winked and breezed by, three blue plates balanced on her arm.

Luke Kayenta's eyes returned to Kitty. Yes, she realized, she still garnered more of his attention than either his food or the swing of Alice's hips. But he had noticed the swing.

"You have fine friends here, I think, Kitty," he said.

She shrugged. "We go back."

"How far?"

"Way before the war. My first job was here at the Westminster, night shift setting up and bussing tables, then waitressing. Jack Spenser was a regular customer. I spilled cranberry sauce all over his pinstripes. Instead of getting mad, he offered me a job at the factory for my day shift."

"A good choice."

"But that almost lost me my job here."

"You had two jobs?"

"Yes, on the production line, sealing up the perfume bottles with a smudge of wax by day. Right after that shift, I came to the Westminster smelling like "Rapture." Alice and the girls had to wash my hands with lemon juice to keep the perfume scent from getting into the food. My mother bathed them in cold cream overnight."

She held out her hands, palms up, to show him where the lemon juice went, then the cold cream. She did not mean for him to take her hands in his.

"Hazardous duty," he said, as if he saw behind the story, that she needed both jobs, more than she needed to finish high school, because the New York Central had just fired her father, right before his pension would have kicked in.

"Hey," she breathed out, "eat."

He released her hands. "I was listening."

"Finish. Hank's leftovers taste a lot worse cold."

"It all tastes wonderful to me."

"You're feeling better if your appetite is... "

"I am not sick!" he claimed suddenly, as if she'd accused him of a crime.

"Easy, Luke. I didn't say you were. But Jack said you'd had a hard time. In Spain?"

"Yes, of course. I beg your pardon." His skin twitched beside his eye. Kitty looked away. She didn't want to care about his rough time, his wounded eyes. A walk. Alice had suggested a walk.

The new girls were going off the lunch shift as she settled the bill. They looked after Luke while Alice dragged Kitty into the ladies' room and its long, fancy beveled mirrors in need of cleaning.

"What a dreamboat! Where did you find him, Kitty?"

"I'm just baby-sitting for Jack."

"That's no baby. Talk about tall, dark and handsome! And Luke's got eyes like Valentino."

"Valentino's long gone."

Alice frowned. "Hey, can't you give the guy a break?"

"You're doing fine for me."

"Hey, what's that supposed to mean?"

Kitty tried to laugh as she adjusted her picture hat. "You fed him half the kitchen."

Alice pinned a few escaped strands back into her upswept hair. "So, I like to watch a nice fella eat. You used to, too, the way I remember it." She stopped, turned sideways, facing Kitty and not their reflections. "Listen, kiddo. You think you're the only one with war troubles?"

"I didn't say anything…"

"You don't have to." Alice's voice softened. "You're wearing those troubles, my friend. Say, where are your stockings? Of all days not to wear those great French…"

"They're in my pocketbook."

"Oh?" Alice's brows disappeared into her curly bangs.

"'Oh,' nothing! We were, um… climbing."

"Whatever you say." Alice returned her attention to her own reflection. "A mountain man, is he? Bet he's got the touch to send you climbing toward—"

"Alice!"

"Put your stockings back on. They look swell when you dance."

"We're not going dancing."

"But you always take Jack's strays dancing."

"That was… before."

"Before one was such a dish?"

Kitty sighed, rooted around her pocketbook. Alice held up the hems of her skirt as she slipped on her garter belt, gathered her stockings, rolled them up her leg, and secured them. Kitty's hands felt cold against her own skin. Would she ever feel warm, feel cherished again?

Alice skimmed her finger along Kitty's calf. "There, the seams are straight. Luke's a leg man, in case you didn't notice that, either." Alice dug into her apron pocket. "Try this lipstick. Matches your shoes better."

"Will you stop it?"

"Nope. A swipe, across the bottom lip, then smudge, like I showed you when we was kids. Just for old times, there's the girl."

Kitty felt too disconnected from the old times now, too different to show a decent guy a day out.

As they swung through the ladies' room door, Luke Kayenta stood where they'd left him, in the middle of a gaggle of waitresses, holding his hat between those nervous fingers.

Kitty cut through, taking his hand. He looked relieved, even rescued. Why? Surely girls swarmed around him at home, too.

She took him to the park. The closest to sheep she could find for him were the long horned antelopes at the zoo. Luke Kayenta seemed uneasy there, too, until he noticed the storybook figures, and all the children playing around them.

"This is for them, the young ones, this place," he said.

"Well, sure. It's a zoo." Maybe they called it something else in Spain? "Zoological gardens," she tried. "Where they keep animals."

"Yes. I know what a zoo is."

Not confusion, then? Queasiness? Was that the reason he looked so unsettled? Did he wolf down Hank's leftovers too fast?

They walked on. His gaze finally settled on a little girl clutching her doll tight, there, outside the panther's cage. A taller boy growled at her ear, then waited for her shrieks. Kitty stepped closer to Luke.

"What's wrong?"

He dead-sighted her, searching, reaching a place deeper than she wanted any man to go. "It's hard to watch them in pain," he said.

"She's not in pain. Her brother's trying to scare her, that's all."

"I mean the cats." He nodded toward the cage. "I think he was almost mad before they brought her to him."

"Her?"

"Yes, the sleeping one. Now he lives only for her, for the young."

"Young? Luke, what are you talking about? There aren't any..."

"At harvest time. September, I think."

How did he know the sleeping panther was female? Kitty thought of the place inside her, the empty place where her baby had been. Could he see there, too? Crazy thought.

"I liked to watch cats at home," Luke said quietly. "I used to station myself on a ledge above them. Watching. I'm sorry, Kitty," he said, looking away as his grip on the iron railing tightened, "this is not a good place for me."

"Rumplemeyer's," she whispered the spot Alice had suggested, and where Kitty often took her niece and nephews after a day at the zoo. "It's not far from here. We'll go to Rumplemeyers."

His more familiar, baffled look steadied her. Had she glimpsed something howling to get out of him, too? Yes, she knew howling. Ice cream. She would feed it ice cream.

At Rumplemeyer's Kitty slid into an oilcloth covered booth as the late afternoon sun slanted in though the windows. They were the only patrons.

It was "you'll spoil their dinner" time for children. Above them, leaded glass patches of cobalt blue and ruby red shone like in church. Instead of saints, a toy drum, a tin soldier, a carousel horse.

It was a good thing the stained glass panels didn't need much upkeep, and still looked beautiful. Below them, the large plate glass windows were not shining with the gleaming clarity Kitty remembered from her childhood. The dulled brass of the fountain showed the high turnover of Mr. Rumplemeyer's running-off-to-war soda jerks, too. As did the dust on the stuffed toy animals still peeking down over shelves throughout. But, even dulled and untidy, Rumplemeyer's was still her family's place, in her city.

Kitty frowned. Her plan to cheer him up wasn't working. Luke Kayenta looked even more uncomfortable as he slid a dripping hot fudge sundae to the middle of the table.

* * *

Luke tried to breathe deeply, but he knew she saw his uneasiness, and was frowning at him again. He'd offended her. Luke couldn't seem to stop offending this woman. Earlier, as he was searching the menu, she'd chosen something for him. The smell of it turned his stomach. But he couldn't tell her, it wouldn't be polite.

"It's un-American not to like ice cream," she said. Her voice was light, teasing, but something snapped inside him.

"I suppose I am not much of an American, then," he said.

"No," she countered uneasily, "you're from Spain."

He heaved a sigh.

"Aren't you?"

"No."

"But— well, where are your wildcats?"

"Arizona."

"You're American?"

He scanned the red leather of the close space containing them -- booth, she called it. Was she challenging him too? The way they all had? Even after the words of his elders: 'We stand ready as we did in 1918, to aid and defend our government and constitution against all subversive and armed conflict.' They'd declared it before the attack on Pearl Harbor, and even earlier, before the state laws of Arizona even allowed his people to vote. Was this woman questioning his loyalty?

"I was born within one of the United States," he said, daring her.

She blinked, then flashed a smile, startling him. "Arizona, huh? Way out west. You're a cowboy?"

He flinched. "No," he ground out between his teeth.

Her smile faded, the rare smile. Why did he drive away her smile? She did not mean to offend him. But no one was permitted to call him a cowboy.

"How ever did you find Jack Spenser?" she asked.

"I did not find him. He found me. As he found you, and made your fingers smell of his business." He glanced down at his hands. "It is the same with mine."

His hands were shaking, again. Staring at them would not stop it. They needed a ceremony. Who in these city canyons could perform one for him?

Luke thought of the eagle feather resting over his heart. There, let his thought of it slow everything down, bring him peace. Even for a moment, even in this place, even with this woman, mourning her man, her child. Jack Spenser had told him that the airman's wife had lost her growing inside child soon after her man had died. There were two holes in her heart, then. She was out of balance too. They were both war casualties, he and the widow.

Why was he telling her the truth about himself? It only bewildered her.

The big man who reminded Luke of his sergeant at boot camp and smelled most heavily of cream, loomed over them both now.

"Our Kitty, you will treat her with respect!"

"Yes, sir," Luke agreed, almost saluting.

The proprietor assessed him quickly, then smiled. "On leave, yes? Used to following orders. He'll follow yours, Kitty." He patted Luke's shoulder. "Try this, soldier." He left a tall glass and returned to his counter.

"Sorry," Kitty said.

Luke stared down his new antagonist -- another confection contained in gleaming, clear glass. Bubbling, white.

"Kitty," he said quietly, "this drink?"

"It's an egg cream."

"Eggs? Cream?"

"No, no, there are no eggs or cream in it."

"Why is it white?"

"That's from milk."

"Milk."

"From cows. I know, your mortal enemies, not-a-cowboy? Aw, try it, Luke. An egg cream is mostly seltzer."

"Seltzer."

"Yeah. You know, a two-cent plain?"

"Phosphate?"

"That's right, phosphate. Now," she slid the tall glass closer, "try."

He did.

"Like it?"

"It likes me," he admitted with a small grunt as he caught another scent from the glass.

"Vanilla?"

"Yes, there's vanilla in it. Say, are you going to finish the hot fudge sundae?"

"No. Would you like to eat it?"

"If you insist," she said, quickly replacing her emptied dish with his. He remembered the ice cream they made all the students eat on Christmas at the boarding school. He had thought it was punishment, because it made most of them sick. He watched Kitty's eyes close in delight as she took in another spoonful. This woman thrived on it.

Luke shook his head. "So much is outside my understanding. I suppose that goes with everything else about your city."

"New York is that mysterious?"

"It is. You are." There. Her light flower scent intensified. And the ghost of the smile that he suspected once lived there on her mouth appeared. He looked down at his hands. "I like mysteries."

He felt the sun now make a streak across his face. Warm, like in the canyons of home in late afternoon. But here it came through colored glass. Painting him, he imagined, like one of the Old Ones, before a battle. He looked up at the woman across the table.

There, in the eyes of the airman's wife. Discovery.

"Luke. You're an Indian."

"Dinè," he said quietly. "My people are the Dinè."

"Din...?"

"Navajo," he tried.

* * *

Kitty had heard of Navajos. She'd seen some in a movie house newsreel about the Grand Canyon once -- dark people with heads wrapped in scarves. They were making rugs, herding sheep. Herding sheep. Of course. That's why he was desperate for the Central Park Sheep Meadow to live up to its name. He was looking for home.

Luke Kayenta was so still that the light's red streak did not move. War paint, like in the movies of Indians fighting the cavalry. Kitty looked past him. Mr. Rumplemeyer stood behind his fancy counter with its soda contraptions, nodding his approval, as if the man sitting across the table was the boy next door in a Judy Garland musical, and not one of the red savages that Errol Flynn and John Wayne killed by the dozen.

Kitty thought of Luke Kayenta's rapt attention; to her, to his food, to the panthers. He began to come together, to make sense. Her fingers whitened around the thick, cold soda fountain glass. No, nothing was allowed to make sense. Break him up again.

Rumplemeyer's front window now had that eagle-eyed attention of his. His expression went suddenly taut, trapped. Then he became a blur of movement as he leapt over the table.

She felt herself slide under him, felt the steel hardness of his arms shielding her, and that empty space inside her. Kitty remembered all those thoughts jumbling through her head as the window shattered with the sound of bursting gun fire.

Chapter 3

Her ears rang, the only sound there beneath Luke on the black and white tiled floor. Had the world caved in? Was she hurt? His scent: wild, now spiced with vanilla. Luke Kayenta shifted and a hunk of cobalt blue glass from Rumplemeyer's window slid into her lap. Dark drops splashed across its surface, then slid off, staining her dress. Blood. Whose blood?

Kitty blinked. Smoke. Get out. They must get out. But the table was above them. And she was so cold. Luke breathed into her hair, her scalp. Thawing her.

His hands gripped her shoulders. Those sharp, steady eyes scanned her face, her crumpled torso. Then his consideration spiraled out, checking her extremities, she realized. Kitty felt no pain. So it was not her blood. It was his.

Sirens pierced the heavy rancid air. Then screams, cries from the street. Kitty saw a flash of two blue-uniformed cops through the shattered window.

Luke's hand clamped over her mouth before she could yell to them -- big, strong, but soft. His other hand pressed against that place inside his coat, his beautiful linen vest. The sound he made as he pressed was like a leaking radiator in the dead of winter.

Valentino eyes, darting, directing them out towards the back door. Alice must have been right about those eyes' effect, how else would Kitty be leading him, crawling through broken glass, then into the alley behind Rumplemeyer's?

"You need a doctor," she told him when they got there.

He shook his head. "A quiet room, water."

"That's a train ride away. Can you. . .?"

"Yes."

When they reached the subway stairs he hesitated, looking more terrified of those steps than about what had just happened to them.

He searched her eyes. "Under the ground?"

"That's where the trains run, rube."

A blonde rushed past, bumping into his elbow. The woman's clutched bag of Quaker corn meal sprung a leak, sending a gold trail down the steps.

Luke watched the trail, then grunted his agreement quietly. His hold on Kitty's arm became more steady.

Kitty banished the insistent questions from her mind and poured all her energy into getting him home. When she inserted the token and helped him through the turnstile, they suffered a few looks and a grin from a passing marine.

"Going in the service, brother?" the marine asked.

Luke smiled vaguely.

"That's what I thought. Listen, pilgrim, the night's young. Easy on the hooch. Show your gal a good time first if you want them perfumed letters while you're gone."

Kitty took Luke's elbow. Others were watching them now. "Good advice, ya big lug," she chastised. "Buck up!"

Once on the Eighth Avenue line car, amusement remained on most of their fellow straphangers' faces. Kitty brought Luke down gently into the seat beside her, praying he could rise again when they reached the Thirty-fourth Street Station. The red stain was seeping through the weave of his vest. She slipped him a handkerchief, which he took with his left hand, passing it to his right, still tucked between his coat and vest.

"Lug?" he asked.

"Never mind," she advised, close to his ear, like a lover's whisper. He looked terrible. Without thinking, she brought his head down to her shoulder. "Rest."

At her stop, he stood slowly, but without her help. Kitty felt more of his weight as they reached the stairs.

"Almost there," she tried to assure him.

"To the above world."

"That's right. And another climb. I'm in a walk-up."

"Walk-up?"

"Building with no elevator."

"We are going to your place?" The eyes began darting.

"Easy. No one is following us, Luke."

He turned, leaning his shoulder against the tiles of the station wall. "Maybe you should leave me here, Kitty," he breathed out.

"No deal. I was paid good money to entertain you. Though I wasn't counting on some crazy Lucky Luciano shooting up Rumplemeyer's."

His eyes nailed her. "There could have been children in there."

"I know," she agreed softly. "But there weren't. It was just us and Mr. Rumplemeyer. Hey," she realized, "I didn't see him at all, did you? Do you suppose he's all right?"

Luke shifted his gaze to the light coming down the last set of subway stairs. "He did not need us," he said.

Well, that was a relief, anyway, Kitty thought. Never mind, for now. She'd get the details out of him once they were on her turf.

He stopped on the fifth step of the station's stairs, breathing hard.

"Come on, Empire State Building man," she coaxed, "you can make it."

* * *

The above world. Luke could see its light. She would get him there. Then he must leave her. She should not be in danger, no matter what level OSS she was. But his thinking was muddled. And she was taking such good care of him.

The air. When the air was around him again, when he could see the sky, he would know what to do.

Outside, he lightened his hold on the airman's wife. The numbers of the streets were lower; 34, 33. This was good. He could find Isaiah Morgenstern, if he walked south until the numbers ran out, and the names began. If he could get out of this woman's grip. But his forehead was resting against the curve where her neck met her shoulder, and she was clucking at him, like a hen to her chick, as he barely kept pace with her steps.

He was so concentrating on their steps together that he missed hearing the new ones.

"Kitty Berry, what is it you're dragging home to your mother now?"

Adrenaline surged into Luke's veins as he lifted his head and looked up at the solid wall of blue uniform.

"We're hardly disturbing the peace, Sergeant Nolan," Kitty answered, sounding more annoyed that frightened.

"And have I remained alive in this neighborhood by not keeping my eyes keen on future rabble-rousers?"

The policeman was armed with a holstered pistol in plain sight, and carried a battle club as well. He talked too fast, like Kitty, but with a different rhythm. Luke disliked him. Deeply, in his bones. And though his hand felt as if it was on fire and the glass fragments ate into his middle's muscle wall with every step, Luke was sure he could kill this man before he'd even thought of raising that battle club.

Stop it. Breathe. The pain and his intense thirst were giving him these thoughts. Balance.

Where was the steady beat of his grandfather's watch?

Gone.

He panicked just as Kitty's fingers spread out across his back, restoring him.

But the one she called Sergeant Nolan remained planted in their path, all blue and brass and armed and too much like the blue-coated soldiers that had led his ancestors on the Long Walk.

"Listen, Sergeant, this is a friend of Mickey's," Kitty spoke up, a fine defiance in her voice, "bringing home word of him to Mama and Papa."

Nolan frowned at him. "You're not from this neighborhood. How do you know Mickey?" he demanded.

"I travel."

"Oh, a wise guy."

"No, not wise," Luke admitted, confused.

Kitty's fingers pressed his back. Luke felt the tips of her nails. "He's a rube from way out west, Sergeant... you know, where Mickey's stationed," she said. "He's not giving you lip, honest."

This language Luke thought he knew as well as his own was now too difficult. He could only maintain his stare. A bad behavior among his own people. And the uniformed man was not even looking into his eyes. But Luke stared because he knew belegaana men hate it.

"Out west, is it now?" Nolan asked, his eyes narrowing. He nodded toward Luke's protected middle. "And takin' on one of your pal's leftover fights, were you?"

"No, sir!" Kitty claimed. "He didn't even know the fella who came at him. There was this marine uptown you see..."

"Jesus, Mary, and Joseph, a marine went after you? Why?"

Nolan's head cocked, looking under the hat whose wide brim gave Luke's eyes shade. "Hey. You a Jap or something? Is that why the Marine went after you? Mickey ain't got the sense God gave a flea. Did he mix in with one of them California Japs snuck out of their camps?"

Luke maintained his expression, and the stare.

"He's American, Sergeant," the airman's wife said for him. "In the service, like I told you."

So. She knew that, Luke thought. Or did she think he was lying about being in Jack Spenser's business?

"Are you, boy?" Nolan asked. "In service?"

"Yes."

"You're out of uniform."

"Yes."

The policeman backed up a step. "So. Mickey all right out there?"

Luke closed his eyes slowly, praying for a vision. He got one. "He is all right."

Nolan grunted. "Not likely. He's no different from what he was here: trouble, like all the Berrys. Uniform or no uniform. Aw, go on, then," he dismissed them. "And keep your nose clean around here, recruit."

"Captain," Luke said.

The patrolman's lips thinned, went white. "What was that?"

"I'm a captain."

Sergeant Nolan looked to Kitty, growling. She smiled. A beautiful smile, wasted on this man, Luke decided. "Mama's waiting her goulash for us, Sergeant. You know how she likes to feed Joe and Mickey's service friends. Especially officers."

"Your mother's gray with the troubles brought on by the pack of you, that's what I know, Kitty Berry," he proclaimed, twirling his polished battle club and catching it twice before finally leaving the street's corner.

* * *

Kitty got him inside her building, where Luke Kayenta's quiet voice reverberated off the tin walls, the black and white tiled floor of the vestibule, a large space, empty of everything but its built-in stone benches and a couple of kids bikes and trikes.

"Kitty, why did you say...?"

"Me?" she countered. "I wasn't the one who became an armchair general!"

"Captain," he corrected her. "That's all I have to give them. Name. Rank. Not reaching into my head for a vision of your brother in his bunk, playing poker for Havana cigars."

"What are you talking about?"

His eyes closed. He swallowed. "Rules of war. All I have to say. Name. Rank."

"You are a captain?"

"Yes." He searched her face. "At Spenser International. They have not cleared you? Even at Level One?"

"Level—?"

The backstairs door to the vestibule opened and the charwoman Mrs. Belkin shuffled in with her mop and pail.

Holy Hannah, Kitty thought. No time for explanations to that busybody. She pulled Luke into the darkest corner of the six corner room. He gave out a little yelp.

She smothered it, kissing him. Hard.

Luke made a deep sound. Kitty felt his vest's watch chain between them. His hand covered hers as he ran his tongue over her moist top lip.

Yes, she thought. That was all she thought. Yes.

He teased the curve of her face and neck with short blasts of air that made her gasp in sudden, ferocious pleasure. Her head fell back under his attentions and she felt her breasts responding.

Alive. So, she was alive, after all.

"Darn kids need to put their trikes down cellar on cleaning day," Mrs. Belkin groused. "I have a mind to…"

What was he doing? What was she doing?

Behind them, the charwoman's footsteps advanced. Luke said something in that language that wasn't Spanish, then swooped in on Kitty's mouth. Deeply.

The footsteps hesitated. "Course, I could always start my duties at the end of the block and hope it's clear later." Then the footsteps tramped for the front door in double time.

Kitty felt Luke's lashes graze her cheek. Long, dark lashes, like women would die to have, he had. That big hand skimmed her hip in a short caress before he stepped back.

"She's gone," he said.

She rocked back on her heels, regaining her balance. "Come upstairs. Let's see to you. Then you're going to tell me why you're not so crazy about the company of policemen, aren't you?"

"No."

She took his hand for the five flights home.

Chapter 4

Kitty hardly saw his gullet move as he poured water down his throat. He took a long breath.

"More, please?" he asked.

She poured him a glassful, then another. "Hey, slow down, you're going to . . ."

She was going to say "get sick," when he did, leaning over her kitchen sink and emptying half of the water he'd inhaled back into her plumbing. Some of it was tinged white; he'd kept his food down, but the milk of his egg cream came up. She wet a clean dishrag and wiped his face.

"I'm sorry," he whispered, his voice thready.

"It's all right. You drank too fast, that's all."

She led him to the big overstuffed chair where she had listened to The Green Hornet and Burns and Allen with Philippe. Luke slid into its comfort as Kitty sat on the arm above him.

"A good place you have, Kitty," he said. His left hand landed on her thigh, patted it. She was not sure he knew what he was touching. She did, and her reaction filled her with touches of other times. And guilt.

"Thanks."

She slid out from under that hand. "Now, stay put."

She felt him watch her every move: back to the sink, to the stool, to the cupboard above which she reached for a bowl, iodine, bandaging, and the tweezers she kept to yank Coney Island Boardwalk splinters out of Zala and the boys' feet.

When she turned, Luke was rising from the chair, not an easy thing to do, even for the able-bodied, which was exactly why she'd put him there.

"I can..."

She pushed his shoulder back before parking her first aid kit on the chair's big flat-surfaced arm. "Show me that hand," she demanded in a voice like her mother's.

He slowly dislodged it from inside his stained vest. The knuckles were chipped, as if he'd been in a poolroom fight. Small wounds were still oozing blood from the imbedded shards of glass. Kitty turned his hand slowly, examining the other side. No wounds there. But there was more to his injuries, she was sure of it. But he was wary and skittish. Well, the hand was a start.

As she picked out the glass, Luke's breathing stayed steady, spiked by small grunts when the tweezers found a long shard. Okay. Maybe now was a good time, she told herself.

"How's the gut?" she asked quietly.

Silence.

She swallowed hard. "Luke, are you shot?"

"I don't think so."

But that's where the rest of his hurt was, his gut, she felt sure.

"It's not so bad," he promised. "If you'll give me those prongs—"

"Nothing doing," she warned. "I patched up my brothers plenty after fights. You're in good hands."

"I know, but..."

"Two brothers. Lifeguards at Coney Island, now both in the navy. Mickey, out in California, and Joe, up in Seattle," she chatted away as she wound the gauze around his hand. "Mickey's boys Matty and Dominic are no angels either. And my sister Anya's girl Zala? That girl can find trouble. So I've seen plenty, don't you worry about me."

Kitty lifted his fine linen coat off his shoulders, her hands gliding past the bulge of a holster. A shoulder holster, like the G-men wore in the movies. Why was he wearing a gun?

She thought of the look in his eyes before the shooting. Was it understanding? Did he somehow know the guys who shot up Rumplemeyer's? How?

She unbuttoned his vest. His fancy fob and chain lead to a blood-stained pocket. Kitty pulled the chain gently. It was attached to what had been an old pocket watch. Now it was a dented wreck in her hand.

When Luke Kayenta saw it, the first sound of real pain finally came out of him. "It is broken?" he asked.

"Broken? Kitty shook it, listened. "I'd say dead." She laughed, then regretted it immediately when the devastated look on his face intensified.

"Time, that is, exact time, confuses us," he said, the words catching in his throat. "We watch the sun." He sped ahead now, talking faster than Kitty thought he could. "We watch the sun, and the task, where I come from, not the clock, you see?

She gave it to me, said it had power and would help me keep together in the white people's world. What will I do now?"

"Easy, Luke. Slow down. Who gave it to you?"

"My grandmother. It belonged to the one she lost, who was her husband."

"Your grandfather?"

"Yes. He was a soldier, in the last war in Europe. She said she saw me following him: towards the rising sun, then the setting one. She said that I would need his watch."

"Listen to me." Kitty showed him the dented case. "Something hit it, see?" "Something that might have killed you today. You did need it."

The frantic look eased, but the misery remained. The watch felt warm in her palm.

"Did your grandfather die in the last war?" she asked quietly.

"No. Later. At home, of the influenza that killed so many. But he had run a good race. The women: my mother and grandmother, remember him."

"Luke, I spoke too fast."

He nodded. "Yes. Always."

"I mean about your watch. Maybe it can be fixed. On the lower East Side, they've got some great watchmakers there."

"Yes. I know one. Down where the numbers are all used up, and the streets have names again. I will find him." His head went back against the cushion. "When I can get out of this chair."

Kitty placed his watch in the ashtray, which she'd cleaned after her father's last visit, and enjoyed his cigar there in that chair. Her father's working life had revolved around the exact timetables of the New York Central Railroad. Kitty laughed. A small laugh, but real. "And in the meantime, I'll keep you on schedule, all right?"

"All right."

"Well, that's settled. Now, let me check the rest of you."

"Kitty, please..."

"Hush," she demanded. "Try to relax."

He obeyed as she unbuttoned his shirt. It, like his vest, had tiny rips through its fine weave, and red stains around them. Kitty used warm water to dislodge the fabric. No fresh blood. That was good. She could do this.

His deep, even breathing wafted through her hair. Calming her, as it did when she was in a panic, after the shooting. But doing something else too, this time.

Because the truth was, Luke Kayenta wasn't a brother or nephew she was patching up. She'd already kissed him like a dance hall hussy. Kissed a man who packed a firearm and was a captain in some damned branch of the service. Kissed him deep and long and hard.

Once she lifted the soft cotton of his undershirt, all thought, and even her guilt about the kissing, evaporated.

"Holy Mother of God," she whispered. She looked up.

He murmured, quiet and comforting, as if someone else bore the horrible scars. "They don't hurt so much anymore."

"When did this happen?" she whispered.

"Winter."

She reached up instinctively, feeling his forehead. It was creased with a thin line of sweat, but still cool. "I'm getting the whiskey," she told him.

"I don't drink."

"It's for me, sport."

"Kitty. If you will let me..."

"Are you right-handed? Left?"

"Both."

"Nice try."

"No, not a try. The truth."

The scar tissue of the even, methodical wounds was red and winding, delicate. The large, ugly patch, high on his nearly hairless chest spread out, like a spill. Was that a burn? Not from a scalding, she'd seen scalding water scars. This looked deeper, and deliberate. So this was what Jack Spenser had called his "hard time of it in Spain?" Several of the scars had been ripped through by the shattered glass of Rumplemeyer's. Wounds going through wounds. A doctor would ask about them. Was that why he wouldn't agree to be cared for by one? Kitty couldn't imagine what had made the scars through his tanned skin, but she had to distract herself with a belt of whisky.

Keep everything clean, she kept reminding herself as she worked. Concentrate, because you owe this man. He is the reason glass isn't now in you. When she couldn't find any more slivers, she put the tweezers down and reached for the gauze. The old and new injuries disappeared behind the white she wove around his middle. Kitty began to feel better.

"One last wrap. How you doing, cowboy?" she asked.

That flash of anger she wanted came into his eyes. "Sheep," he corrected though his clenched teeth, "I herded sheep."

"You mean 'This here's cattle country, get them sheep out of here.' Like in the movies?"

Gentle amusement lit his face. "Yes. Just like the movies," he said right before his head fell forward and he passed out.

She ran into the kitchen for fresh water.

"Luke," she called, pressing the wet cloth at his temple and sounding calmer than she felt, "Open your eyes."

Those audacious lashes flickered.

Kitty held the water glass to his lips. "Sip. That's it, good. We're all done, all done now," she crooned, as if he was little Matty and the boardwalk splinters were out after a day at the beach.

He touched her cheek with those long fingers and smiled. "It ends in beauty," he said.

"There will be no endings in my place. No more endings," she told him sternly.

"One more," he insisted. "Why I came here. Why I came to you. I'm sorry. One more."

"What are you talking about?"

He reached his good hand into his vest, which was lying there on the chair's arm. Toward that holster, his gun. Oh God, she thought. He was too good to be true from the start. He was one of those gangsters. She'd misjudged him badly.

And after that soft, polite apology, he was going to kill her.

Chapter 5

Kitty always thought she'd be able to scream at a moment like that, scream good and feisty like Fay Wray as King Kong approached. But, she'd learned better at Rumplemeyer's. She was frozen now, too. She stared at him, not believing that the serene face before her could bring death.

He reached past the holster and pulled out a battered white envelope.

He offered it to her like the priest offers Holy Communion, at her chin. On it was written her full name: Katherine Barichievich Charente. Her maiden name was not shortened to Berry, like her West Side neighborhood knew it.

That's not what started her trembling. It was the handwriting: large, flamboyant, with its loops and flourishes. A barnstorming pilot's handwriting. Philippe's.

"Where did you get this?" she demanded.

"I promised to deliver it to your hands. Your hands, only. Not give it to the censors to pore over. I trusted an honorable man, and the love he had for you. I do not care what they do to me for bringing it to you. I promised."

Kitty crushed the envelope between her breasts and reached a shaking hand to clear back a thatch of his black hair.

"You're in the intelligence service?"

"Yes."

"So is Jack Spenser, isn't he?"

Luke didn't answer. Kitty remembered all the times Philippe would touch the end of her nose when her questions about why a Canadian pilot member of the Royal Air Force spent so much time at a perfume company. "There's no need-to-know for you about that, Kitty." That's what Luke was doing now, in his silence. One of the things she'd found terribly glamorous about Philippe now enraged her.

"My husband, he is dead?" she asked in a furious whisper. She didn't realize she still doubted it until that moment.

"Yes. I'm sorry."

"They didn't bring him home. They didn't bring anything of him home."

"At a place where a mountain touches the sky I buried him. I will show you the place. There's no grave mark, but I remember. When the war is over, I will show you."

Kitty had worked for Jack Spenser for years. He had trusted her with his switchboard, with his strays. This stray had shattered Jack's image like the shots had made short work of Rumplemeyer's window.

Luke's voice pulled her back to her present. "I will go, Kitty. If I can rest a little while here, then I'll go away."

She pulled her red leather hassock up to the chair and sat. She unlaced Luke's shoes, removed them, and propped his feet up. "I'll say who stays or goes in this joint, shepherd."

She gathered her mother's large, spider web-patterned shawl from the back of the couch and spread it over him. "Now, rest."

He closed his eyes. His even breathing was a comfort, somehow, as she sat on the edge of the couch staring at the envelope, trying to find the courage to open it. She brought it to the kitchen, where she caught a glimpse of her stained dress in the window's reflection. She dropped the letter on the table. The stain would set if she didn't take the dress off, soak it in cold water.

She did that, after wrapping herself in a dressing gown.

Then she brought out sheets for the couch, and a light summer blanket. She returned to her bedroom, opened her bottom drawer and pulled out Philippe's nightshirt, the one she used to wear when he was away. The one she still wore. Its cotton was soft and faded. She placed it on the couch. For Luke, when he woke.

Kitty returned to the kitchen table. The battered envelope was still there. So was the whiskey. She'd only downed a thimble full before she'd cared for Luke's wounds. Someone had left her the whiskey after the funeral. It was less than half full. It was all the hard liquor she had in the house. It would have to be enough.

Finally, under the pool of light cast by the wall sconce, she finished a glassful, then another before she opened Philippe's letter.

Its first pages were written on creamy stationery with a linen weave. It had been crushed, battered, folded, but never torn. Philippe was particular about stationery, and pens. His favorite was an old reservoir type that had belonged to his grandfather, a Quebec country doctor. The message her husband had written with that pen put him in the apartment with her.

Kitty read neatly spaced words of devotion, love, of hope for the holy possibility that had been growing in her. Philippe's formal, serious, writing self was in that letter. That Philippe quoted Shakespeare and Voltaire and John Donne on death and its sting.

The last page of the letter was shockingly different—scrawled in pencil on thin blue airmail onionskin. Still, the labored handwriting, smeared, and with the ghost of a splattered stain underneath it, was his.

Jack and the representatives of the Royal Air Force told her he'd died in performance of his duty. Instantly, they'd said. Another lie. He was dying when he wrote this, she thought.

"Darling Kitty," she read.

Trust the one who gives this to you. He has cared for me at great risk to himself. I almost expect him to sprout wings in the slanting sunlight. Take all the comfort you can from what I wrote earlier. Let the rest go. It was written by a man who did not know grace until you. He, like me, loves you madly. Always.

Kitty pressed her hand tight over her mouth as she finished reading. She shoved the letter in a kitchen drawer, under the linens. There. Now she was free of its finality, free to weep until dawn.

But no tears came. She fought the urge to wake Luke Kayenta, who had seen her husband out of his life, and beg for every detail.

She didn't have to wake him. The telephone did.

Kitty bolted up, crossing into her living room, reaching for the phone in the middle of the second ring.

Luke Kayenta's good hand covered hers before she lifted the receiver.

"I am not here," he said at her ear.

Third ring.

She felt the barrel of a gun between her ribs.

She nodded.

The iodine-scented fingers of his right hand shifted the receiver slightly so that they both could hear.

"Kitty? Jack. Good, you're home. How did everything go?"

She glanced quickly into Luke's strained face. "Oh, we had a swell time."

"And our man behaved himself?"

"Sure. A perfect gentleman."

The feel of the gun barrel eased.

"Where did you go?"

"Empire State Building, lunch at the Westminster, the zoo..."

She heard Jack's laughter. "So, we not only found the only choirboy in our business for you, but he was a cheap date besides?"

"It's the only way I like them, boss."

"I owe you."

"You're right."

A pause. "Kitty," Jack broke the silence. "Might you come in tomorrow? I know it's Saturday but, for an hour or so, early? It will mean a new position with us, if you want it."

She slid a look at Luke Kayenta, who nodded. "All right," she agreed.

"Great. We'll get you back home before those relatives of yours starts knocking at your door for weekend breakfast."

"They don't knock."

She heard her boss's easy laugh. "I'll send a car over at seven."

"A car?"

"No more subways for you, my dear. Did I say it was a promotion?"

"I'll be waiting downstairs."

"Good girl. You sound tired. Get some sleep. I'll see you in the morning."

Kitty replaced the telephone receiver. Luke released her.

She whirled on him, and his gun.

"Put that away," she demanded.

* * *

Luke looked down at his hand, holding the gun on this woman who had been so good to him. He had responded to his training. Deep shame wrapped him like a cloud over the moon. "The safety was on. I could not have fired it," he tried to explain. "Kitty..."

"Away. Now." Her mouth was a hard line of displeasure.

He snapped the weapon back into its holster, knowing from living with women that she was not nearly finished scolding him.

"I didn't cover for you because you threatened me like...like a thug."

Thug. A blunt, ugly word that stuck in the throat. He didn't know what it meant, but it made him want to show her his bare neck, like contrite Coyote in the stories.

"I did it because of the letter," she continued, the heartbreak entering her tone. "Only because of the letter."

"Thank you."

"Thank Philippe."

"I thank you both."

"Stop it!"

"What?"

"Stop confusing me!"

Her shout sent him back a step. He ran his good hand through his hair. "Confusion will get worse once Jack makes you Level One," he warned her.

"Is that what he's up to? Enlisting me?"

"I think so."

"Will the lies stop then, at least?"

How could he explain the service to her, when he was still struggling to understand it himself? "We try not to tell lies. Not complete ones. We allow people to make assumptions, based on what they see, what they think they know. That is how the operations work best. I was a shepherd at home, so I was one in Spain. It worked, for a while."

"The scars. They're from burns? Torture?"

He nodded. Her questions did not stop.

"Your partner, the one you climbed the Empire State Building for... hey," she warned, "keep looking at me."

He thought he would fall if he did, from being so out of balance, and without his grandfather's watch to steady him. But she was doing it, he realized, she was steadying him with those determined eyes.

"He died there," she said slowly. "In Spain. Like Philippe."

"Yes."

"Jack Spenser sent people to their deaths?"

"Nobody sent us, Kitty. It is dangerous work. We were volunteers. We knew what we were getting into. And we were out of uniform."

"But Spain is a neutral country."

"With close ties to the Nazis."

"Nazis gave you those scars?"

"No. They had not gotten their turn yet."

"They killed Philippe."

"Yes, he was in the middle of a mission, and they shot him over France. But he made it over the mountains, he made it to us. His plane went on, finished the task. Your husband, he moved their secrets along, and saved other lives, Kitty. And he died in grace and beauty, only worried about his letter getting to you."

"Suffering? In pain?"

"Yes. For a little while."

"How little? How long, damn you!"

"A few hours, on morphine. Then, enough time to finish his letter. I did my best for him. I'm sorry. Kitty, I'm so sorry."

"They killed him, and your friend. Why didn't they kill you?"

His eyes took refuge in a gilt framed photograph of a man and woman sitting in an old model Ford hanging in a place of honor on her wall, a wall papered with images of trellised roses, before he returned his attention to her face. "I can't tell you that, Kitty."

"They wanted something, didn't they?" she persisted. "Did they get what they wanted?"

He could tell her that much. "No."

"You didn't lie then, to Sergeant Nolan. You're a captain."

"I did not lie. But I did a foolish thing. Because of that contempt on his face. I have seen it many times, I should be used to it. I should have let him believe what he wanted to. That truth might have been a mistake."

"Why?"

"Because I don't know who my enemies are."

"Enemies? Here? Listen, Nolan might take a bribe or two from the numbers guys, but he's not even jealous of men in the army, like most of the overage flatfoots. Nolan's just a beat cop, Luke."

"Beat?"

"Yeah. Our neighborhood is his beat, his territory."

What had he done, Luke thought, staring at the red of her lips. He had tasted her, touched her like a man touches a woman who has wrapped herself around his heart. He had done these things in this territory, this beat, her home territory.

"Nolan will know that I was here. So will the woman with the mop. I was not thinking, coming up here with you. Here, to your rooms, your place. I did not think about others, talking, in a bad way, about you. I'm very sorry, Kitty, I was not thinking."

She shook her head, smiled. Was she still as angry with him if she could smile in that way that turned him inside out?

"Aw, relax. About that, I mean. I'm a big girl, you lug."

Now he was a lug again, that word she'd called him when they were in the train that ran under the ground. It did not sound as ugly as putting that tongue-to-teeth sound before it — thug. And the way she said the word had a smile behind it, that went nicely with the color at her cheeks.

"My whole family lives in this building," she said now. "Mom and Pop will cover for you, say you're my brother Mickey's friend, just like I did. If they like you."

"Will they?"

"Sure. You were Philippe's friend, and Philippe became their son when I married him. So. We will all be close to the truth." The dark lashes of her eyelids descended as she frowned. "Like you being a Spanish shepherd selling perfume"

"I was selling rugs."

"Rugs? Oh, Jack," she said, coming toward him, and not seeming angry at all with him any more.

* * *

Kitty felt herself drifting toward him, pulled by Valentino eyes and the whiskey.

"There. Enough fretting about my lost virtue, at least." She touched his forehead.

A muscle in his jaw jumped.

"Do you feel hot?" she asked.

"No."

Kitty almost laughed. He was blushing. And breathing in the most delicious way against her throat. They were too close. But she had started it. Again. Her fingers pressed harder and picked up the throbbing at his temple.

"You're a little warm," she pronounced, trying to sound like her mother. But Mrs. Berry wouldn't be drunk, as Mrs. Charente was. Drunk and off kilter with grief and leering like a B-girl at his uneasiness. Enjoying it. What was wrong with her? This was not who she was. But was anything going to be the same, after this day?

His left hand cupped her face, while his thumb traced a path down her cheeks. Slowly. What was he looking for? The widow's tears she had not shed?

She stepped back from that hand, from those slightly flared nostrils, from his iodine and sage scent. Because she wanted to protect him, even more than she wanted this.

"Luke. Why do you want to hide from Jack? Come in to the office with me, tomorrow. Let's tell him what happened at Rumplemeyer's."

"No. They promised a furlough, after my debriefing. Well, I need a furlough here, now. Give me until you return from your meeting, Kitty, please. That long to think this through."

"I must be crazy. But I need to check Jack's story. And find out what he wants of me. So, all right."

"Deal?"

Kitty smiled. "Yes. Deal."

She nodded toward the sheets and light blanket. She picked up Philippe's folded nightshirt, remembering what this man had done for her husband. That and the deepening darkness outside, those things seemed to be making up her mind for her, not any good sense. She put the nightshirt into his hands. "Bathroom's on the right. Get out of those clothes while I make up the couch. Then, sleep."

His eyes softened. "You, too."

"You'll stay?" she demanded, but softly. "You'll be here when I get back from meeting with Jack? So we can talk over everything?"

"I will be here."

That didn't sound like one of his half-truths. It sounded like a promise.

She left the glass paned French doors between her bedroom and the living room open a little, just enough so she wouldn't disturb him when she left in the morning.

Kitty woke after a night of dreamless peace. Her mother said she was her best sleeper, and best eater. Even with an armed Indian on the couch, Ma, she wanted to tell her.

In the early light, Kitty watched Luke's sleeping reflection as she pinned on her hat in the hallway mirror. A small, tight-fitting hat, with a veil. A hat that matched her burgundy suit, and said she had a serious, responsible job. Behind her,

Luke Kayenta filled out Philippe's nightshirt a lot differently. His leg was bent and resting against the back of the couch, tenting the blanket. His arm was drawn across his eyes. A breeze wafted in from the fire escape. Luke opened his bandaged hand to it and smiled, looking like that choirboy Jack called him, or maybe like the angel her husband mistook him for.

It was a comfort to her, thinking that maybe Luke Kayenta's eyes were the last sight of the world Philippe had.

How was Jack's story about Philippe's death going to compare to Luke's own? If they were very different, which should she believe?

Well, one thing at a time. It was Jack's turn, Kitty thought as she opened her apartment's front door. She'd be listening for the partial truths, thanks to the man sleeping on her couch, who told more than a share of his own.

Chapter 6

Jack sent Gus, his personal driver, who had always been polite to Kitty over the years. That politeness remained, but Kitty caught a hint of disapproval too, like a scent, in small gestures: a hard-slammed door, the tug on the brim of his cap, hiding his eyes. Did she notice a bulge under the arm of his uniform coat? Was it like Luke's? Or was she seeing armed spies everywhere?

At Spenser International, only a few lights guided them through to Jack's large, gleaming, modern office. Gus left her there.

Jack's Swiss-made clock and elegant French pen holder were the familiar anchors at each end of his desk, but something was different. No papers, receiving orders, notes. She had never seen Jack's desk clean before. The mahogany top shone. And he wasn't behind it.

"Thank you for coming, Kitty."

Startled, she turned. His light gray suit, his stillness, made him almost invisible against his floor to ceiling silver blinds. He strode to her side, took her hand. Not to shake, but to hold, to give a gentle squeeze, the way he'd done when offering condolences.

"What's going on, Jack?"

His attention went to a window. Long, sleek. With a heart-stopping view of the greatest city in the world.

Kitty wanted to see his eyes. Her mother said people's eyes don't lie. "You wanted to become more a part of Philippe's world, didn't you Kitty?" he asked the empty street below.

"Yes. You know I did."

"You are in the shell of it. That's what Spenser has been, since before the war, the shell around some privately generated intelligence operations. We were struggling to catch up with the British then. We still are, the truth be known... spying has never been this country's strong suit. But all wars are wars of information as well as battles. The international reach of my family business is a good cover. So, we're now part of the new branch of service, with a new name: the Office of Strategic Services."

Kitty touched his sleeve. She needed to see his eyes. He turned. "I wanted to tell you this before," he said, "but I'd promised Philippe."

"What did you promise?"

"That you'd stay what you are—my crackerjack receptionist and a charming companion to agents on furlough, but no more than that. He wanted you here, but secure, for him to come home to."

"He's not coming home," Kitty said, the hollowness of the words taking on a new depth, now that she'd read the letter.

Jack nodded. A few strands of his thinning, silver hair fell across his forehead. He slicked them back impatiently. "That's why it's now time to give you this choice. Kitty, back when you were on the factory line, waxing over the top of perfume bottles, I remember thinking: this young one will come of age in a safer world. I never thought we'd get ourselves into a worse scrape than last time. But here we are, sacrificing another generation. Yours."

"Is Luke a sacrifice?"

The lines around Jack's mouth deepened. "Let's go back a bit. Luke's just returned from an assignment in Spain, as I told you." Her mind alerted to a half-truth. "You may have gathered that he's not Spanish. He's an American Indian, Kitty, of the Navajo tribe."

Kitty felt a trickle of sweat on the back of her neck. "A Navajo," she repeated. She didn't like this business already.

"Kitty, you don't know what desolate means until you've seen his home. He and some kind of cousin of his, they showed up at our recruiting station, carrying rifles that dated back to the Spanish American War. So eager, the both of them.

"Luke had been off the reservation at least, with a couple of years of college. And he is a natural leader." Jack sounded like a proud godfather now, like when he talked about her and Philippe, and how he'd brought together the match of his fledglings.

"If we can get this project going on a larger scale," he continued, "we'll need many more of the Navajo. We'll need Luke for that. It has to work!"

He met her direct gaze and heaved a sigh. "They were on a trial run with a new intelligence project when our two Navajo were captured, imprisoned, there in Spain. We lost his cousin. Some of our men don't trust Luke now. They want to sacrifice the project. But I never doubted Luke's loyalty to us, to our country and the mission. Especially after…"

He stopped, resuming his study of the hazy early morning.

Oh, no you don't, Jack Spenser, Kitty thought. Tell me the rest. Tell me how my husband really died: stranded, abandoned, in agony.

"After what, Jack?"

"After the service Luke has already rendered."

That was all she was going to get out of him. Not how, not where, no offer to take her to Philippe's grave, after the war.

"Our allies, the ones that Luke helped, they praised him to the skies," Jack continued.

And her husband thought him an angel. Kitty wanted to know more, to learn who had given him those scars. She kept silent, fearing she'd give something away, even the affection she was feeling. Jack would use it to find out more, she thought, as he turned his attention to the precise movements of the clock on his desk.

"He's just a kid, really," Jack said. "He should finish his education and become a teacher or doctor working to get his people out of the dark ages. I hope he gets the chance. Truly I do. But right now, we need him."

Kitty had seldom seen Jack like this: with his sophistication, his urbanity stripped away. He took a long breath.

"The OSS is filled with human beings, Kitty, just like any other institution. We're fallible, with old prejudices. Some look only at Luke Kayenta's race, and at the Indians' long wars with the United States. Some resent that he is intelligent, and sober, and holds his head high, a walking contradiction of their expectations.

"I liked him from the start. But we lost his partner in an escape mission, then almost lost Luke in another. We need to know if their project's been compromised."

Kitty thought of how her mind had at first refused to make sense of Luke's scars and the cruelty that had caused them. She thought of the letter Luke Kayenta would not surrender to his boss, only to her. How did he get it out of the place where they did such terrible things to him?

Philippe's letter was hers alone. She took a strange pride in that, though it made his death more real.

Suddenly, she caught a scent of that mixture of motor oil and sweat and sandalwood that was Philippe. She pulled it into her lungs. Too fast, too desperate, the way Luke drank the water from her sink.

"Kitty? Do you need to sit?" Jack asked.

"No." She stood taller, realizing a pain was creeping up from the back of her head. She should have asked Gus to stop for coffee. And some aspirin tablets. The hangover from last night's whiskey had very bad timing.

"Go on, Jack," she whispered.

"Luke looked so worn out yesterday, and a special agent was late for our appointment with him. When Luke asked for you, I thought the least I could do was offer him an excursion before his debriefing."

"Why did he ask for me?"

"I don't know, but I wanted to give him a good welcome home."

She'd hardly welcomed him home with the grace she'd always found for Philippe. There was the scent again. Philippe.

Kitty imagined him cradling the back of her head, as he'd done once, when she had the flu, his hands so comforting. Would her husband want her here? The one who wrote the first part of the letter would not. But what about the other, the one whose searing pain was in every scratch on onionskin?

"What would I be doing, if I decide to...enlist, is it?"

Jack smiled. "Yes, that's it exactly, just like the other service branches. Listen, do you like Luke a bit, Kitty?"

"Well, he grew on me."

"Good. He's not a worldly man, he shouldn't suspect."

"Suspect what?"

"That he's your first assignment. First we'll keep our missed appointment. I promised Dr. Saltzman he can have a crack at Luke. But after that you take over and..."

"Dr. Saltzman? A crack?"

Jack smiled. Why? Did he have an inkling that she liked Luke, more than a bit? "The good doctor is a psychiatrist on call for our service. He'll help Luke with that jumpiness. You noticed it, remember? After Dr. Saltzman does his assessment, we'll send Luke back to you. He might tell you things he won't tell us."

"What things?"

Kitty noticed a small scar she'd never seen before, to the side of Jack's mouth. It met a natural crease, extended it. These men and their secrets, their scars, she thought.

"Don't worry. We'll guide you if you decide to join us. Once you do, there will be training, and you'll be an officer. Your outward job will still be at the switchboard. Not even your family must know."

"And if I don't want to enlist?"

"You'll have a job here as long as you'd like, Kitty. Strictly perfume-related."

Kitty felt cold, suddenly. She was already keeping two secrets from her boss. What happened at Rumplemeyers, and that Luke Kayenta was sleeping in her living room. Her relatives would be invading her apartment in a couple of hours. Could Luke still be one of Jack's strays to her family? One who got a little too drunk and she'd let sleep it off on her couch? Another lie in this structure of deceit. Necessary, in wartime. Necessary, she told the pain that was rising up the back of her skull and now invading her stomach.

Jack took her hand. "You need time?" he asked.

"Yes, time."

"Of course. I'm rushing you, because you always felt like part of the team, and I'd be honored if you started climbing levels with us. Take the weekend to decide."

"All right," Kitty agreed.

But she'd already made up her mind. Philippe and the baby were dead. She still had a family, that she'd already put at risk for a man who held a gun at her side. He'd shielded her from harm too, and he kissed like a rocket to the moon.

But she already knew something Jack didn't. Luke Kayenta wasn't in that hotel room. And she surmised he had no immediate plans of meeting with Jack Spenser, or a fancy head-shrinker. Not after the attack on Rumplemeyer's.

Sure, she owed the guy sleeping on her couch, because of the letter. But she needed to send him on his way, with one more secret, and she needed to go back to her job at the switchboard.

* * *

After Kitty Charente left her home with a click and soft bolt latching the door behind her, Luke Kayenta dreamed he was asleep in a cave beside a sacred cottonwood grove, with the spider people spinning stories all winter long. He picked up the sound of the stories--soft, gentle murmuring.

He then remembered where he was and wondered if the murmurings were the dreams of the other people sleeping in this many floored house, one like those the pueblo people lived in. They must have been good dreams because he slept better than before he went down hard on the beach at San Sebastian with his dying clan brother on his back.

Luke felt the sunlight on his eyelids. Perhaps he should sing Kitty Charente out of her black as part of his morning prayers. Would that be a good gift? A good trade for what she'd given him?

He had begun to think that he'd stopped feeling at all. When the glass flew he'd acted on instinct, the one that said: survive. But he was something more too: a protector, of the airman's wife, smelling like an exotic flower from a beautiful place.

When he was near death, the suffering in her husband's light eyes eased only when he spoke of his woman. Luke asked the airman's forgiveness now, as he imagined tying her lush hair with a silver and turquoise ornament. Her hair was as densely black as the women of his country, but full of waves, like a bounding shoreline at night.

Kitty's clothes were different, too -- not calico cottons, like the women at home, but a weave that was soft and supple, that moved like another layer of skin. That he wanted to touch, like a curious child, then like a man. That cloth and her nylon-clad legs set his veins singing.

The airman's wife made him remember he was a man. A woman's man. He was grateful, profoundly grateful, for this gift.

And when they stood in the lobby of her pueblo home, it was she who had kissed him. He knew about kissing, thanks to the flame-haired woman at school who'd taught him what to do with his mouth to please her, to please himself. It was something like the gentle bites and licks between his people, but deeper, more intimate.

Intimate, full of meaning. Meaning for him, he reminded himself, not to that flame-haired woman, not to belegaana, not to Kitty. But was she as hard-hearted as the other? That one had shown him how to dance in their way, and to kiss. She'd allowed him to do many things that pleased them both. But when he came to her house with his courting gifts, she had laughed as her father and brothers beat him. He was only her walk on the wild side, her taste of the other, she'd told him. How dare he even imagine he was courting her?

Luke winced, remembering his humiliation. It set off the pain of the cuts the shattering glass had made. Who were the men with the guns? Who sent them? Stop it, looking for answers without enough information. He was in the information business. He had to find more.

On his own.

And he had to be on guard, looking for more good signs, like the eagle catching the thermal winds on top of the world's tallest building. The eagle left his gift to the window cleaner: a Mohawk, who then gave the eagle's gift to him. Luke had felt the quiet strength of the bird, and of that one he had honored, the one who is not here. They entered him through the gift.

And then, when he was lost and afraid, the stream of cornmeal led him down the steps, underground. And Kitty Charente, the airman's wife, took the letter from his hands, deep in her mourning, but not hating him because he could not save the airman.

Her kissing's were the best sign: easing the trouble that plagued his heart: that he was still alive, when the others were not.

He heard footsteps. Had Kitty returned? No, too many footfalls for one woman. They stopped, outside the door. The quiet voices muted further as a key went in the lock.

Instinctively, Luke turned, pulled the sheet over his head and sighted his pistol as their soft whispering became clear.

"Look, Anya! Kitty's sleeping on the couch again, poor thing!" one woman said.

"Maybe the pipes are clanking, or Old Man Petrov came home drunk below her bedroom again," the other answered.

"Well, maybe, but..."

"Ma!" A child's voice came between the women's.

"Now, nothing more noisy than a game of checkers before Aunt Kitty wakes up, you three," the first woman directed in a lowered voice.

"But Ma, I don't think that's..."

"Enough with the thinking, Zala. Just keep the boys quiet. Tell Aunt Kitty we'll be back around noon. And don't touch the stove."

Luke heard the door close again.

Three sets of light footsteps approached, but not too close to the couch where he lay. Children on a rabbit hunt, he thought. And he was the rabbit.

"Zala," one whispered. "That's not Aunt Kitty's hand."

"I know."

"Is Uncle Phil still dead?"

"Yeah."

"That couldn't be him then, right?"

"Right."

The footsteps came closer.

"Could it be his ghost?"

"Nah. Ghosts are invisible."

"Unless they have sheets over them."

"Oh, true."

Luke heard one brave set of footfalls continue an advance on the couch.

"Look, his fingers-- bandaged. Ghosts can't hurt themselves."

"That's right!"

"Shake him, Matty."

"You shake him!"

This was ridiculous, Luke thought. How could he ease out of his cocoon without making things worse between him and these children?

He stretched slowly. The sheet fell away, drifting to the floor. He opened his eyes.

Two boys in short pants, their hair slicked back, perhaps six and eight, were huddled under a taller girl's arm. All had scurried back against the front door.

Now they were the rabbits.

"Good morning," he said quietly.

Only the girl found a voice. She stood tall and straight, a protective little mother. "Morning. Where's Aunt Kitty?"

"She was called into her work place. She'll be back soon."

The smaller boy eased out from under the girl's arm. Her hand stayed on his shoulder. "Are you a ghost?" he whispered.

"No. I'm Luke."

"You're hurt. Is Aunt Kitty hurt too?"

"No. She took care of me."

The girl smiled slowly. "She's good at that. So's Gram."

The smaller boy still looked wary. Luke opened his good hand to him, showing the palm, as he would do with a frightened dog at home. "Are you hungry?" he asked his rabbits.

"Yeah."

The other boy tilted his head. "How about you, Mister?"

"Yes. Very hungry."

The children looked to each other, nodding, appearing satisfied. They knew ghosts didn't have much of an appetite, Luke surmised. So he asked them to find the largest frying pan in the kitchen, to start a breakfast.

Chapter 7

Kitty asked Gus to leave her off at the corner grocery, so she could get a pound of bacon and a loaf of Silvercup bread. She even splurged on a couple of oranges, to make juice, knowing that Luke was not going to deplete her milk supply. Strange, knowing such an intimate thing about him already— that he was probably allergic to milk.

She couldn't think too hard about it. That would make her head feel even worse than it did. Just send him off after a decent breakfast, she told herself. She wasn't taking the job. Let Jack find someone else to watch over Luke Kayenta.

Watch over, nuts. Spy. She was nobody's snitch.

Mrs. Kosovich, the grocer's wife in her blue flowered apron, knew a hangover when she saw one. She insisted on making one of her herbs-and-raw egg concoctions. As she eyed Kitty downing it, she chanted to whatever old country goddess was in charge of foolish people who drank too much.

"Gah!"

"There's fire left in your eyes," Mrs. Kosovich pronounced. "So. He was a good catch, the one in the nice suit you were kissing?"

Kitty frowned. "Mrs. Belkin should mind her own business."

"Say that when you're in her circumstances, Kitty Berry! Ten buildings she cleans every day, too exhausted for a life of her own. Say that when your rent's not paid up a year in advance by a man in another nice suit."

Anger cleared Kitty's head better than the remedy. "You think I wouldn't scrub floors to have my husband and child back?"

Mrs. Kosovich flinched, hand rising to her own throat.

Kitty walked out of the shop, slamming the door. How did Mrs. Kosovich know Jack had paid a year in advance on her apartment after Philippe died? Probably from Anya, her own sister. Kitty sighed. Sometimes she hated living in this fishbowl neighborhood.

Once inside 442, she climbed the stairs to her apartment, led by the scent of something sweet. Maybe Mrs. Cruger, forever hunting in her Dutch grandmother's attic upstate, had discovered a new doughnut recipe. The scent grew more intense, making her mouth water. Her climb turned into a sprint. As she fumbled for her keys, the door swung open. Zala almost knocked her over.

"Aunt Kitty! What'd you bring us?" Anya's daughter poked into the grocery bag. "Mmm—oranges, Grandma!" she reported back to the original Katherine Berry.

Kitty's mind froze in panic as she remembered promising to look after her niece and nephews this morning, early, so her sister and sister-in-law could catch the sales. She couldn't move. Her mother walked into the living room, wiping her hands on a dishrag.

"I forgot. About Anya and Molly dropping the kids over this morning. Mama, I'm so sorry. I forgot."

Her mother shook her head, smiling, serene, her top-knotted hair slightly askew.

"Luke told us you was at work," Molly's Dominic said, ducking out from under her mother's arm and showing his double dimples, "so we didn't worry about you."

"Yeah, Luke minded us good, Aunt Kitty," she heard Matty call from the kitchen.

Dazed, she patted Dom's head as he took the bag of groceries from her arms. Then she followed him around the corner to the kitchen, her mother and Zala following.

Luke Kayenta stood at the stove, his vest and shirt covered by her plainest white apron. No sign of his holster, his tie, his formal suit coat. His bandaged fingers and hand were the only tokens of the day before.

He held her iron frying pan in his better hand, while his fork turned something that looked like a jellyfish from a bad day at Coney Island. Matty climbed on a stool at Luke's elbow. "Come on over! You gotta watch this, Aunt Kitty!" he proclaimed.

When the glob hit the sizzling oil, it blew up, turned golden, and smelled like heaven. That's where the scent was coming from: her kitchen, her frying pan.

Her mother retrieved the towel from Luke's shoulder.

"Good! I think I got that turn of the wrist now, motka. I'll finish this batch."

Kitty's eyes met her mother's. Motka. She was calling him God's gift.

Luke Kayenta's smile traveled all the way to those Valentino eyes as he nodded a greeting in Kitty's direction.

"Welcome home," he said.

* * *

All the strength that his full night's sleep and her family's good company had given Luke began to drain from his bones. His offerings were not pleasing her. Kitty sat, staring into her cup of coffee. Was she angry?

He didn't know what to do, so he was glad when her brother's smaller son, the one his grandmother said had been vaccinated with a phonograph needle, plunged in between them. "When Grandma smelled Luke's fry bread, she came down to trade some for her sinkers. Right, Grandma?"

"That's right, Matty," Mrs. Berry said from her place at the stove.

Luke patted his middle, where he'd put too many of the balls of cake and nuts and dried fruit. "It was a good trade," he said.

Kitty's mother smiled. Luke liked Mrs. Berry, Lady Liberty's rival in her husband's affections. She resembled the copper woman in the harbor, he thought, with her proud stance and generous lap, with room for many children. Her silver hair and soft, deep-set eyes reminded him of those of his own mother and grandmother, who also wore their hair knotted, but lower, and wrapped in their sheep's woven wool cloth.

Mrs. Berry had been full of welcome, and she had not asked him as many questions as his mother would have if she'd found a strange man in his sister's hogan. For that Luke felt grateful.

"Dominic," Mrs. Berry summoned her older grandson now, "run up and ask Grandpa to find you some powdered sugar in the cupboard above the sink. That will finish these beauties off nice."

"Yes, Ma'am," Dominic replied.

The boy turned back at the door. "Grandpa won't talk to Luke too much, will he? Me and Matty and Zala want to show him our pigeon coop on the roof."

Something happened then, between mother and daughter's eyes. A narrowing of vision which both did in exactly the same way. A signal. Luke felt a constriction within his ribs. But Mrs. Berry's eyes remained soft as she spoke again to her grandson.

"You're right, too much talking is possible when we haul your grandfather into our breakfast party. And you and Matty and Zala will soon have to start trying on clothes your mothers' found at the Saturday bargain tables, too. Better take Luke up into the fresh air now, first. The sugar can wait."

Matty beamed. He was the younger, one dimple brother. "Come on, Luke! Before Gram's sinkers start weighing you down to the floor."

The older woman began unlacing Luke from the apron. He looked to Kitty, letting his eyes ask -- does this have your permission?

She stirred her coffee, shrugged, and then granted him a small smile. Perhaps she was not so angry with him? As he turned, the tips of her fingers touched his elbow, sending a pleasant charge through him.

"Be careful moving," she said.

"I will," he assured her, lingering under the warmth of those fingers until he felt the tug at his shirtsleeve from Matty, heard the girl Zala's giggle.

Mrs. Berry folded his apron over her arm. "You have younger brothers, Luke?" she asked.

"No, I am the youngest of our mother's children. But I have nephews." He spread open the fingers of his bandaged hand, showing Kitty their dexterity. "Five. Three sons of two sisters. And two nieces." He thought of the boys, tending the family's diminished herd without his help. Well. Better there than where he had been. He found himself caught in the depths of the woman's kind eyes and felt compelled to say more. "I hope the war does not last long enough to touch our young ones."

"From your lips to the ear of God, son," Mrs. Berry assured him, before Zala, Dom and Matty pulled him into the hallway.

* * *

"Poor boy," her mother said, as the door closed. "He has seen too much of this war already."

Kitty blinked. Her mother had gypsy blood. There was no use in hiding from her. "Mama, let me explain some things about Luke."

"Explain while you eat," she summoned, pouring coffee. "And talk fast, we'll need to defend your stray when your father comes barreling in here."

"Luke is Jack's stray. And he has to go."

"Go? Go? What are you saying? The Romanian with his squealing violin all hours of the night, that crazy Mrs. Amarin with the baby-biting dog, they should go from this building. Luke serves our country, looks at you like the queen of the May, and makes for the children doughnuts... no, no, what does he call it, fry bread," she reminded herself. "And he ate three of my sinkers besides! So. Your Luke. He can stay. If he gets past your papa's eye, of course."

"Why do we need to bring Pop into this?"

"There is no 'bringing' milada, not in this building. Eat. Then tell me what kind of trouble Luke is in. And what happened at Rumplmeyer's."

Her head shot up. "Who told you about—?"

"Chew, Kitty, or you'll give yourself the heartburn. When Alice Weiss saw Mr. Rumplemeyer... well, his remains, in the middle of the Daily News photo pages this morning, God rest the poor man , she rushed over, saying she was worried because she'd sent you two over there."

"Mr. Rumplemeyer? He's dead?"

"Two pages, center section, just like in the old days, with those hoodlums."

Kitty sat back. What had Luke said when she'd asked about Mr. Rumplemeyer's condition? "He doesn't need us." Only the look in Luke's eyes said why. She hadn't read that look right.

"Hoodlums?" she repeated, forcing herself to think past what Luke had seen. "Mama, do the police think that? That hoodlums fired on an ice cream parlor?"

Her mother looked out the kitchen window, as if there were someone standing on the stone ledge, listening, before she lowered her voice. "Back in the prohibition times, they say there was a back room speakeasy. Such a small space, hardly a dozen cozy tables." Her mother's eyes darted about the kitchen now. Her parents may have visited this back room before Roosevelt ended prohibition, Kitty thought.

"They say maybe Mr. Rumplemeyer ratted out Alfredo Nunzio back in those days," her mother continued. "And Nunzio just out, under very mysterious circumstances, let me tell you. They had him on three manslaughter charges. He should have been in Sing-Sing for the life of him, that one. At least the police could have warned Mr. Rumplemeyer that Nunzio was out, maybe put some extra men on patrol. A disgrace."

"Did they catch the shooters, Mama?"

"Not yet. But they got it all figured, those boys at The News. Good reporters, ears open at every police precinct, and our Mr. Fellig from the neighborhood selling them the pictures."

She and Luke had been caught in the crossfire of a mob hit, then? With all the evidence pointing that way, would Luke return to his hotel today, before Jack's people came knocking?

Her mother was still speaking.

"So, Alice and me, we come downstairs to check on you. Instead, we find Luke cooking breakfast for Zala and the boys. Alice made poor Luke tired with her questions, her fussing over the bandaged fingers. She was always jealous of your boyfriends, Kitty, you got to watch that one!"

"Mama!" she tried to reprimand, but was glad, for her throbbing head's sake, that at least Alice had gone.

"Did Alice leave the paper, Mama? Did Luke read it?"

"Sure he did. And said you were both there, and that's where he got cut up, but no details, probably on account of the boys were trying to see Mr. Fellig's photographs of Mr. Rumplemeyer over my shoulder, and I said nothing doing, they'll be climbing the walls in their sleep, from seeing that gore. We all said a prayer for the poor man's soul instead. So, Kitty, you're all right?"

"Luke shielded me. Mama, I think he saw it coming."

"Eagle eyes, that boy has."

It was more than that. Had he expected it? But Kitty couldn't tell her gypsy-blooded mother what so troubled her. "He wouldn't go to a doctor," she said instead, "so I had to bring him home."

"Of course you did." Her mother thumped the tabletop with the heel of her hand. "He stays!"

"You don't understand. Jack's not finished with him, and he won't go back."

"So? It's a free country."

"Not for him. He's not a salesman. He's in service, Mama. Like... Philippe was."

"And Jack Spencer? He's their boss?"

"Uh...yes." So much for keeping secrets, Kitty thought with a groan.

"Oh, I knew. Always I knew, what with the two of them, always in the corner talking quiet at our get-togethers. And Luke is our Philippe's friend?"

Kitty thought of her husband's letter, wedged in her kitchen table's drawer. "He was a good friend to Philippe, yes."

"Well. He's family, then. Milada, don't worry so." She was milada, her mother's love, and Luke was God's gift. Kitty frowned at the clear-eyed way her mother saw the world.

Katherine Berry the First, as her father called her mother, went on dispensing thoughts as they occurred to her. "This military is not army, navy, marines. Very loose. Sometimes wear uniform, sometimes don't wear uniform. Men keep crazy hours, in this service. The nylon stockings, they drop from the sky, into pockets of people who are in this service. But this time, the service waits. Our Luke, he visits the pigeons, learns some stoop ball with the boys, then maybe he changes his mind about this reporting in."

That made sense, Kitty realized. The attack on Rumplemeyer's settled old scores from another time. It had nothing to do with Luke's service in Spain, the loss of Philippe and his friend, or his own terrible scars. Maybe he would change his mind, and go back to his hotel.

Kitty breathed a little easier, and finally bit into the confection Luke had shown her mother how to make. Her senses ignited as the light, crisp shell gave way to the airy center. It tasted both like a doughnut and like Christiano's best crusty bread, but better than either. And somehow, he had concocted this confection from her sparsely supplied kitchen. She hoped her mother had memorized both ingredients and technique.

Kitty watched her mother drizzle another piece of fry bread with maple syrup and place it before her.

"Seconds?" she asked lightly.

Kitty dove for it. As she ate, she forced herself to consider what might happen next. Luke would soon report for duty. Then on Monday, she'd refuse Jack's offer, return to her switchboard, nobody's the wiser. Luke would then disappear back into the O.S.S. After the war, he'd find her and keep his promise to show her Philippe's grave. There, done: a plan. If he survived the war himself. Kitty used her pinky to clear the drop of syrup from the corner of her mouth. Her eyes began to smart.

She looked up. Her mother was smiling. Along with her Saturday house dress and apron, she was also wearing a smear of lipstick. Kitty's lipstick.

"He's single, our Luke?"

"I don't know," Kitty realized, surprised by the clutch at her heart.

"He talks of mother, grandmother, sisters, nephews, nieces. No children. No wife. He's single."

Suddenly, the door swung open and her father appeared, framed by the kitchen doorway. Suspenders wove through an old white shirt and held up his Saturday gardening pants. His face wore the disappointing scowl that he'd perfected over years of meeting his daughters' boyfriends.

"Where is he?"

"Good morning, Papa," Kitty tried to back him down with courtesy and his old-country name as she stood.

"No, it is not. Not today," he proclaimed, eyes narrowing behind his rimless spectacles, "It is not a good morning, when the woman who cleans the hallways is telling tales about my daughter and a man."

Kitty felt like emptying Mrs. Belkin's pail over her head.

"Papa, you should eat," her mother urged, pulling out a chair. "And listen to your daughter, not some gossip."

He sniffed at, but refused the fry bread. He sat. Although her mother's hands rubbed his shoulders, his face and mostly baldhead remained flushed red with anger.

Kitty leaned her back against the sink. "I met him at work, Papa. Mr. Spenser asked me to show him around the city, you know how he does that sometimes?"

Her father grunted.

"Well, this man, Luke is his name, he needed..."

"To kiss you in the hallway of the building that is home to the families of your parents and sister and brothers?"

"I kissed him, Pop."

He turned to her mother, his blunt fingers springing out of his fist and pointing toward the ceiling. "You hear this? Your daughter is doing the kissing of strange men."

"He's not strange!" Kitty's voice pitched up in frustration, "He's good and kind and...and far from home, like you were once. And I am not your little girl. I'm the widow of another good man. It's...it's been a long season without rain, Papa."

Her father's nest of dark eyebrows shot up.

"And Luke is a gentleman," she sought to reassure him. "He slept on the couch," she said, hoping she didn't sound as regretful of that fact as she suddenly felt. "Ask Dom and Matty and Zala," she added, triple-daring him to check her story as if she were a sixteen year-old. She watched his frown deepen. She was considering going into the Office of Strategic Services? She couldn't even make a decent man sound decent to her own father.

When the kids and Luke surged into her apartment, even Matty knew to hush.

Luke's smile went crooked but he met her father's intense, direct gaze.

"Mr. Barichievich," he pronounced carefully. She'd only spoken her maiden name once. How did he remember how to pronounce it?

Her father took Luke's offered hand. Slowly, Dominic Barichivich's fierce look dissolved. Then, another miracle: creases appeared at the sober corners of his eyes.

"How big was your last flock?" he asked.

"One hundred and twenty head, sir," Luke answered.

"Good spring?"

"Twenty three births, two sets of twins."

"Lucky."

"Yes. For my people, this is lucky too."

"Any losses to the wolves?"

"Never saw one."

"Not tempted to raid. You did your job well."

"It was not a harsh winter."

Her father tilted his head. "We lived with our sheep on an island in the Adriatic. Not many harsh winters there, but starving times, just the same. You did well by your flock."

"Thank you, sir. But others did most of it. I was away. But I helped with some shearing, where I was, this spring. And the sheep? They did well by us too."

"You are far from your home country, my daughter says."

Luke's glance met hers. Kitty saw no displeasure in it. "Very far," he agreed.

"Who tends your flocks at home?"

"My mother, grandmother, sisters. And the eldest of their children, now."

"With you in service, like our Philippe."

"Yes, sir."

A silence descended between the two men. Kitty thought it safe to speak.

"Pop, I didn't tell you that Luke tended sheep."

"You think one can't tell another? A man's profession gets into his hands."

The softness, Kitty finally realized. Her father's grip had been like steel, before he lost his job on the New York Central line. But thirty years before that, in his old country, he'd once told her how his hands had felt like Luke's did— soft from the lanolin of sheep's wool.

"You are welcome here," her father decreed. He didn't even launch into his usual admonitions about propriety or correct intentions towards his daughter. Or ask if Luke went to church, and which one.

Her father's smile was so wide Kitty saw his gold tooth. "A shepherd," he said, shaking his head. "My youngest daughter brings home a shepherd, here, to the twelfth ward of Manhattan Island, in the city of New York! This is a country worth defending, this America. Anything can happen, here. Go, put your hat on, shepherd. We'll take a nice walk by the river, you and I."

Chapter 8

Luke stood in her bedroom, exhilarated from his time with the children and birds on the open rooftop. His lifted spirits were not even disturbed by the prospect of a walk along the Hudson River, even in the company of her father, who did not yet trust him, but who had been a shepherd, too.

He breathed out the nagging pains at his middle. He breathed in welcome, and Kitty's scent. He traced it to the glass bottle on a mirrored ledge. The ledge was on the right side of two low, shining wooden drawers edged like a waterfall. In between the sets of drawers was a large round mirror, almost as tall as he was. Luke walked over to the extraordinary piece of furniture and took up the bottle, reading its label. Kitty Charente's scent came from Jack Spenser's factory and had a name: Gardenia.

Luke lifted the glass stopper and as he did, caught his own reflection in the mirror, frowning at himself for touching this thing of hers, this female thing, perfume.

He was not used to the reflected sight of himself. Mirrors at home were few and small. He rarely even looked into one when shaving. But while the sheep grazed on the mesas, the Echo People often reflected his voice. Luke was more used to that, his voice singing back at him. Before yesterday, on the Empire State Building, he hadn't heard himself singing much, either. That was part of who he used to be. That was part of himself better in balance.

Luke liked the world of Kitty's giant mirror. Within its frame he saw her bed, covered with an amber cloth that glowed with the light filtering in from the window. It would fit them both, this bed.

Stop. Stop seeing his hands coursing through the black waves of her hair, taking her down on the wide bed, easing his terrible heart sickness in soft places: the curve of her shoulder, her breasts, between her thighs. But he didn't stop. He stayed in the image of the lush richness of her body, his imagination taking their intimacies further. He entered her, feeling her breasts rise, watching her smile. They would fit. She was for him. He was for her. He lived there in his mirror world, feeling her power, her sleek legs moving, her mouth over his, their life breaths mingling.

And then he saw the chindi rising, like a plume of white smoke, from the bed.

He turned, cold with his own fear. Whose chindi was it? Who had died, leaving the evil part of himself here? Was it the airman, angry, jealous that Luke was having such thoughts about the woman who had been his wife?

How could that be? Luke had buried the airman an ocean away, in a place where the earth touched the sky, the sky that Philippe Charente had loved as much as his woman.

It had made Luke feel sick to touch his body, to put it in the earth. The taboos were so strong that the Dinè hired belegaana to bury dead relatives at home. But the airman had no one. So Luke had spared his clan brother all the touching. He'd taken the body through the north facing door of the mountain hut. He'd tried to do everything in the right way. But now his clan brother was dead, and his own life was off the right path, so far off. So the airman's chindi had somehow found him here, maybe. Luke felt his breath being robbed as his ghost sickness intensified.

Stop it. The missionaries said such beliefs were backwards and the work of someone from their own Christian religion, the Devil. But the Dinè had no devils. They were trying to follow a narrow path through a world swarming with supernatural beings. More of the white plumes rose from the bed. A cold fear gripped his wounded middle. Was it as his superiors suspected? After Spain, was he losing his mind?

Luke reached for his pouch, for corn pollen to protect himself. His shaking fingers found the broken watch of his grandfather, who had once lived in this belegaana world of mirrors, of ticking clocks marking time. Then came the airman's voice, complete with its French Canadian lilt. No time for a walk by the river with her father, it said. It was time to go. Where? Another white plume from the bed brought the swift stabbing image of his clan brother, and blood on the beach of San Sebastien. Then the others who'd been killed in the prison intruded. They made his path narrower.

The chindi filled the room, pushing him toward the window, the sky, and madness.

The curtain wafted. Air. Release. Luke approached the window. On the street below he saw Nolan, the policeman. Two others flanked him. Also in blue uniforms, but not buttoned properly. Nolan was talking to Kitty's nephews, who were pulling a red wagon. Luke couldn't hear their talk. Matty crossed his arms. One of the men shoved him hard enough to knock him into the wagon.

Luke fought the urge to fly out the window, like a chindi himself, to haunt this man who would hurt a child.

The three men left the brothers and plunged into the building. Both boys looked up at the window. At him. Luke heard their thought, the same thought as that of the airman's chindi: time to go.

Luke turned, grabbed his shoulder holster from the top of a high chest of drawers and strapped it on. He yanked on his coat, shoving his hat inside his vest before opening the window.

Fifth floor, with a ledge outside. Narrow, but no more narrow than some he'd chanced himself along the canyons at home. It led to the iron platform outside Kitty Charente's larger room, the one she called her living room. The platform had a zig-zag of stairs almost to the street. And his freedom.

Luke looked back inside the bedroom. The chindi were still there. But Luke thought perhaps the white image mirror people were not chindi after all, but were the supernatural beings that the

Dinè and the belegaana religions both had: Chi. Angels.

* * *

Kitty's family and friends never knocked. So she jumped at the rapping at her front door. She'd heard that kind of pounding when Joe or Mickey were in real trouble from the numbers men, or the cops. She approached, but stopped before her hand touched the doorknob.

A second barrage of knocks.

"Who's there?"

"Open up by order of the police."

She glanced back at her parents. Her mother's hand cupped her forehead like the night her brother Joe bested the mayor's nephew in a poolroom fight. Her mother did something else she did then too: posted herself at the bedroom door, folding her arms. Her father's steady hands took Kitty's shoulders. He nodded.

Kitty opened the door to a beefy arm and a billy club.

"You don't have to put another dent in the door, Sergeant Nolan," she said.

He had two cops behind him, but Nolan did all the talking.

"Where is he?"

Her father spoke. "Who is it you are looking for?" he asked in the precise English he used when speaking on the telephone.

Nolan looked from him, to her mother, to Kitty. He smiled without humor. "So, the whole hunyack bunch of youse is hiding that filthy Jew?"

Kitty didn't have to mask her surprise. "Jew?" she repeated.

"Kayenta. Should of heard that Jew boy right in his name."

"Luke? But, Sergeant..."

"All them anarchist Jews can do is throw bombs and run for cover."

"Bombs? What bombs?"

Nolan looked Kitty and her parents over. "Friend of Mickey's he told you, eh? What a load of goulash you dimwits were swallowing!"

Kitty was thinking the same thing about him and his cohorts as they turned to her mother, who blocked the way to the bedroom.

Nolan approached. "They hide behind women's skirts, the Communist Jews. Step aside, Mrs. Berry."

"You have a warrant?" she asked, without moving.

"Don't need one." He grinned wider. "It's wartime," he proclaimed, shoving her aside. He kicked open the door, which was not locked, so the hinge didn't have to break. But it did.

Kitty's bedroom was empty.

"Closet!" Nolan barked.

"I don't have one. Maybe the bathroom?" Kitty suggested.

Nolan's eyes narrowed. "Wising up at last," he complimented her gruffly. "Where is it?"

Kitty pointed. "Off the kitchen."

The men charged out.

Her mother kept watch while Kitty and her father ran to the open bedroom window. She expected to see Luke hanging off the ledge like

Harold Lloyd in an old two reeler. But he was already jumping off the last rung of the fire escape. He paused only to run that big gentle hand through her nephew Matty's hair and then sprinted off across Thirty-third Street.

Chapter 9

The careful grid of Manhattan Island turned into a tangle of winding streets and alleyways. Luke Kayenta watched the sun, to keep his bearings in this endless cliff dweller city.

The people walking around him changed with the scents in the air. Languages and skin tones changed. For a time the walkers were dressed in black cotton and darted about like spiders. Luke felt like a looming giant among them. Then they were taller and carried baskets full of vegetables and yeasty breads and strong smelling cheeses.

Could he find his way back to the airman's wife? Never mind. He had caused her and her people enough trouble. He shouldn't go back, not even in the cover of night, to make sure they were all right. With him gone, Nolan would leave Kitty and her family alone now, wouldn't he? Who were those men? Surely not O.S.S., who were sometimes reckless, but would never shove a child. The child, Matty, fell again in his mind. Stop it. He had checked. The boys were sound, and had shown him the right direction: east.

Had the men followed him? Luke had no sense of them now. What if he couldn't find the address he'd memorized? Where would he go then? Too far ahead, Luke chastised himself. You're thinking like a belegaana, too far ahead. Consider the birds of the air, the lilies of the field, he remembered one of his favorite passages from the belegaanas' own great book, the bible, and found peace there. He asked the maker of that peace to look after Kitty and her family.

Around him, the people changed again. They grew darker, with more hair and beards. Their clothing was darker too. The shops here smelled of dried fish and strong root onions. But they were closed. He remembered that it was Saturday. Sabbath.

Would all the shops be closed? Where would he go then?

Luke picked up the scent of the oil of a fine lubricant. It was drifting up from a small windowed space under the, what did Kitty's nephews call it? The stoop. He looked down at the transom window over the door, and at its number: ninety-six, carefully painted black and lined in gold. Beyond the glass door were countless clocks, mocking his failures in this world of the belagaanas, ruled by time.

Too late, as when the rescue ship left without them. Too late on the beach, trying to staunch the flow of his clan brother's blood. He was always too late.

Luke descended the stone steps and approached the glass door. Behind the counter, his jeweler's loupe to his eye, the man's stillness amid all the ticking, the gears, the pendulums, drew him. The well-oiled door opened without a sound.

The balding man sat in the shop of his father, where he said he would be. He looked better, fuller, stronger then when they were in prison together. Stronger, Luke realized, than he himself felt at this moment.

Luke approached the counter, casting his shadow over the man. A bird squawked. Stationed over the front door, the parrot on a brass swing stretched his yellow wings.

The proprietor smiled. "Only one man could get by Eziechiel."

The loupe dropped into his waiting, steady hand. Isaiah Morgenstern's eyes were as deep and compassionate as Luke remembered, shining through the broken bones, the scars of his years in a Spanish prison. Luke's fingers found the chain of his grandfather's watch. But he could not find his own voice. Only a strange, rough sound came out. Hold out the watch, he told himself, and find your voice.

"It's broken." What was wrong with him? Had he lost the ability to greet his elder properly? Luke blinked to clear his vision, suddenly gone blurred. No good. He blinked again, longer. Worse. Now his face was wet. He should go.

Isaiah Morgenstern took his grandfather's timepiece from his shaking hand.

"I dreamed that you'd come," he said, ignoring Luke's tears. "I wanted that dream to be a prophecy, so I urged it on. Why? Because sometimes fate has to be tempted, my dear Hell Hole bunkie."

Bunkie. One of many strange and wonderful new words Luke had learned from this man.

"Now, how did I urge fate along, you'd like to know?" Isaiah continued, as if their conversation was two-way. "Well, come, see what I buy every market day. Yes! Every day since that dream of you walking into my shop on those cat feet of yours, Lieutenant...no, Captain. You are a captain now. And why not, doesn't that crazy branch of the service have some little sense?"

Isaiah took Luke's arm, led him past the curtained doorway in the back of his shop. "My entire family lived back here, my friend, in my father's workroom, back in 1905 when we fled Odessa's pogroms— riots that killed two sisters who died protecting me. Can you imagine, the five of us who remained, living in this space?" He stopped himself. "But of course you can. You come from a persecuted people, too. Forgive me, my young friend. Come. Come inside."

The back room was large, but without windows, only a single door in the far wall. Where did it lead? To the outside? Was it locked? How secure was it? Light, from above, a window in the ceiling. Another way in, but not out. What was it called, that window? Luke remembered: Skylight.

The warm summer sun shone on the oblong table, its yellow cloth, and a blue bowl of peaches. Their scent filled Luke with longing.

"See?" the man who'd shared a cell with him, but never that story, the story of his brave sisters, now proclaimed. "Peaches! Just what you wanted, more than any other food, when cockroaches were looking good to us! Waiting. For you. Peaches. Sit. Rest. Eat, my friend. I will work on your fine watch. You will tell me about this thorn in your heart. And we will call some friends here. We will gather our allies."

* * *

Kitty's father was outside the closed kitchen door, speaking with a level of desperation she had never heard before, to the two policemen Kitty had never seen before. Because he knew it was never good to be alone with a cop like Nolan. His sons had been in this situation, once or twice. But never a daughter. Here in her now closed off kitchen, the framed photograph of Philippe smashed under Nolan's air raid warden boots.

"You don't have your flyboy to protect you any more. You should be nicer to me."

He approached her, his voice quiet, seething. "Now," he started in his getting-down-to business voice, "Where would he go?"

"I don't know."

Nolan came closer to where he'd placed her, in a kitchen chair in front of her stove. He wove his fingers through the loose waves of the hair at the back of her head. Then closed them into a fist. Kitty heard the ping of three hairpins hitting the linoleum floor. Her mind resisted. This wasn't happening. She snapped to full attention when he thrust that blue uniformed knee between her legs, pushing her thighs apart. The chair tipped. He yanked her head back and pounded it into the stove, once for each word of his repeated question: "Where. Would. He. Go?"

Behind him, Kitty saw the pages of the phone book flutter in the open window's breeze; one of

Matty's baseball cards fell to the floor. She wanted to say "Dumb cop, dumb flatfoot cop," the way her brother Joe said it that night they roughed him up for breaking the mayor's nephew's nose. She was not that brave. But she kept her silence, kept Luke safe. The knee slid her skirt higher. She saw the spit bubble out the side of Nolan's whiskey mouth. Day off, she realized. It must be his day off. He hadn't shaved. She'd never seen him like this. The chair went back too far. She hit the floor. The scent of Luke's fry bread lingered on the edge of the madness.

A bellow burst from Nolan, a sound that made Kitty brace her arms over her head in self-protection. Then her kitchen filled with towering, gray suited men. They knocked Nolan to the floor. Only then did Kitty feel the tears streaking down her face.

The gray suits pulled Nolan and his two cohorts out of her apartment. Jack Spenser remained there, with one other, a very tall man in a navy blue suit. The man stood by the kitchen window, looking out. Jack leaned over her. His eyes were kind. There, deep under his scowl. At least that's what Kitty tried to convince herself.

"Any lasting damage?" he asked her.

"No."

"Get up."

"Jack, my family..."

"Everyone is all right. Come on, Kitty, get up. Let us see that you can do it on your own."

She did. His eyes eased a measure of their worry. He did not touch her. She did not want to be touched. She wanted to be scoured with steel wool. Don't think about it, she warned herself. And don't cry any more. Jack looked around her kitchen, at the broken chair. At the stranger by the window, his back to them. Well over six feet, the man's head reached the top of its frame. He turned. He was a middle-aged man with sharp features, a pointed beard, and a superior air.

"Kitty, this is Dr. Otto Saltzman."

The man bowed, but looked to Jack. "Perhaps I might examine Mrs. Charente for injuries she might have—"

That accent. She backed up a step. "I'm all right, thanks."

Jack held the man at bay with a slight rise of his hand. "Dr. Saltzman is the one I told you about this morning, Kitty. He has special knowledge that might help us."

"I have nothing to say to him." Two could play this game of talking through Jack Spenser.

The man's light eyes narrowed, but did not look surprised or offended. Jack exhaled. "Dr. Saltzman, if you'll wait in the living room for a moment?"

"Of course."

Kitty listened for the man's footsteps before she spoke. "He's German," she said.

Jack sighed. "Based in Chicago for years. Escaped Hitler and his Nazis back in the thirties. Comes highly recommended by our midwest people. And Dr. Saltzman has more levels of clearance than you have at the moment."

"So he's the head doctor?"

"One with special knowledge of American Indians. He has studied the culture and customs of the Southwest tribes."

"And now wants to put Luke under his microscope?"

Jack's scowl deepened. "Would you mind leaving that decision to..."

"Yes, I'd mind it plenty. If you thought Luke Kayenta was crazy, why in hell did you involve me in all this?"

"You were supposed to tour the city, not bring him home, attach him to your kith and kin!"

"That couldn't be helped."

"All right, I understand."

But he wasn't admitting defeat, only switching gears. Kitty had seen her boss operate long enough to know that. She didn't like being on the receiving end of it.

"Philippe would kill me for this," Jack said quietly.

"Philippe got us into this."

"What?"

Kitty lowered her voice. "Did you ever wonder why Luke asked for me to be his tour guide? He'd never laid eyes on me!"

"Yes, he had."

"When?"

"Last winter. The night of the Guggenheim party, the night before Philippe flew them all to England for training. Luke saw you and Philippe saying your goodbyes on the airfield."

"He... didn't tell me that," Kitty admitted. "Jack. Philippe trusted Luke Kayenta with a letter.

Luke hid it. God knows where he hid it, but he kept it safe and he delivered it to me."

"What are you talking about?"

Kitty didn't like the look in Jack's eyes now, thinking she was hysterical, doubting her word. She pulled open the kitchen table drawer, dug under the linens, the soup ladle, yanked Philippe's letter out, and shoved it at him. "Here. You and your German doctor want to inspect it for state secrets? Go on. I saw it first, it's part of me now. Luke kept a promise to a stranger he buried in the mountains of Spain. Not one who died instantly, over France. Liar."

Jack said nothing as he opened the many folds, read the contents of Philippe's goodbye. Calmly. Everything her boss did was so damned calm. Kitty ran her hands over her arms. Her mother's soft weeping beyond the door cut through the buzzing at her ears.

"Jack. I need to tell them I'm all right."

He looked up from the letter. "So, convince me first."

"What did Nolan and his thugs think they were doing? Why do they think Luke is a communist? A Jew?"

"That is none of your concern!"

There. A hint of passion out of him. Well, she could match it.

"No? Look around. Kicking my home to pieces and terrorizing my family— that's made it my concern!"

He breathed out. "Our concern," he conceded. "Listen, about Philippe's death. We were trying to spare you pain."

He carefully re-folded the letter. "If I return this to you, without filing any kind of report on it, will you allow us to ask you a few questions?"

Kitty took his offering, stashed it back in her drawer. "Yes."

Dr. Saltzman returned to the kitchen upon Jack's summons. He gave her a grim, thin-lipped smile. She knew his type from her waitressing days—- fastidious, demanding, poor tipper. There was a line of brown in his silvery tie that bothered her. A stain. He righted, then sat on the kitchen chair that had a splintered back, thanks to Nolan. She wished she hadn't agreed to this.

Jack began. "Kitty, what else did Luke tell you?"

"More than you were willing to spill when I was sent to show a Spanish salesman the city."

Her boss had the grace to wince. "I never said he was Spanish. And need I remind you of our previous meeting this morning? And that you neglected to mention a machine gun raid on an ice cream parlor?"

"Try not to look away when you are hiding something, Mrs. Charente," Dr. Saltzman advised in a flat monotone. "It is the mark of an amateur."

Kitty shifted her gaze to him. "I am an amateur." She turned to her boss. "Jack..."

"Imagine my surprise at being the last to know," Jack said, annoyed. "It's why we arrived here at a good time for you."

We. Jack and his doctor and his gray suits were not on a rescue mission, then. "Mama did not call you? You were coming for Luke, weren't you?"

"Once we checked the hotel and found he had not shown up."

"Why so many of you? To be ready to take him by force, if he wasn't ready to speak with your head shrinker?"

Jack frowned deeply as he exhaled. "Kitty. Circumstances, and some bad judgment on my part have put you into this situation much deeper than you were meant to be."

"You're not answering my question."

"Mrs. Charente," Dr. Saltzman said, "if this project has been compromised..."

"Answer my question." She stared at each man in turn.

"Yes," Jack Spenser finally admitted, "we would have taken him by force."

"And you wonder why he's not on your doorstep? Look what you sent us into!"

Jack placed his hand over hers. "We thought you'd be safe, Kitty. You've got to believe that."

"Why? Why do I have to believe anything? Who were those men with the machine guns?" She was sounding like a petulant child, Kitty realized. It made Dr. Saltzman visibly bristle. She didn't care about him or his special knowledge into Luke's head. But she was sorry for her outburst as she watched Jack's shoulders sag under burdens she was only beginning to understand.

"Good God, if we could untangle our internal disputes long enough to fight the Nazis and Japanese, we'd have a chance to win this war." He ran his hand through his hair, a young, uncharacteristic gesture. "You know, new operatives usually give me a little time to think I'm in charge."

Kitty smiled. "Sorry, boss."

"Kitty, listen to me. You don't know anything about the man!"

"He protected me. At Rumplemeyer's. He got me out of the way of those shots."

The doctor's placid expression changed slightly. "You believe the fire was aimed at you, Mrs. Charente?"

Kitty felt herself shaking, as she realized it might have been true.

"Possible," Jack said slowly. "Going through you to get to him."

"Who? And why did they kill Mr. Rumplemeyer, Jack? Was he coming to help us?"

"Mrs. Charente." The doctor's condescending smile was worse than his frown. "Do you understand how far you are out of your depth?"

"About as far as you're out of Luke's trust, I'd guess. Listen, you'll have to let me try to find him on my own. I'll talk to him about coming back. That's all I can promise."

"I must advise against this," the doctor said evenly. "If Captain Kayenta is unstable, he might be dangerous."

"Not to me, Dr. Saltzman. I don't know much, but I know that much. It's you two who'd better watch your backs."

Chapter 10

Matty worked silently at her side, holding the dustpan as Kitty swept broken glass into it.

"What kind of trouble is Luke in, Aunt Kitty?" he finally asked her.

"I'm not sure," she told him.

He emptied the dustpan into the kitchen trash bin. "Did he do something bad?"

Kitty stood the broom against the ice box. "No."

She took the baseball card from her apron pocket. "Hey, kiddo. Look what I found."

Matty shoved his hands in his pockets. "Aw, Luke never even saw a baseball card before. Didn't know whose picture was on that one. What a rube, huh? Me and Dom and Zala, we had to explain to him that Lou died last summer, and now the Yankees are in a fix without him. Luke won the card off of me, fair and square, playing checkers, while you were out. He could of kept it."

The summer sun shone through her kitchen curtains, making the top of her nephew's tousled dark hair gleam with red highlights, a gift of his second generation Irish mother. "Matty, when I was gone, did Luke talk to you about anyone, maybe a watchmaker?"

"No. Just Mr. Morgenstern."

"Mr. Morgenstern?"

"Yeah, his friend."

"Morgenstern." Kitty grabbed the phone directory, flipping to the M section. There were three pages of Morgensterns. Matty watched her, his head quirked sideways. She took a deep breath. "Did he say anything else about Mr. Morgenstern?"

"No. He talked about trees next."

"Trees?"

"Yeah. Said he learned from you that there weren't any sheep in the sheep meadow, so he figured there wasn't an orchard on Orchard Street either, except maybe long ago. Me and Dom and Zala, we said we didn't know, that Orchard Street was on the Lower East side, where Gramps goes to get his hats in Jew Town, but we never went with him."

Orchard Street. Kitty's finger traveled down the page. Morgenstern and Son, Watchmakers and Repairs, listed on Orchard Street.

"Aunt Kitty?" her nephew called her attention out of the book.

"Yeah?"

"Is that where he went? Is Sergeant Nolan right? Is Luke a filthy communist?"

She put the phone book aside, and took her nephew's shoulders. "Matty, listen to me. We're all Americans. You, me, Luke and Luke's friends. Sergeant Nolan too, even if he'd like to kick a lot of us out."

"Or just kick," her nephew whispered, looking at the broken glass in her garbage pail. "Did he hurt you, Aunt Kitty?"

"Or just kick," she agreed, realizing her nephew was on the verge of tears. "Not much hurt, Matty. You?"

"Same. I'm tough!"

"Me, too." The ache at her scalp intensified. Kitty wanted to take her nephew into her lap. When had he gotten too big for that? Matty put on that cocky smile, the one he'd gotten honestly from her handsome, trouble-prone brother.

"We're glad you and Luke work for Mr. Spenser, Aunt Kitty. His fellas can rough up cops!"

"Not all cops," she corrected. "Bad cops, doing bad things. Listen. Can you and Zala and Dom look after Grandma and Gramps for me?"

"You going to find Luke?"

She touched his nose, the way Philippe used to do to her. "Now, there's no need-to-know for you on that," she said quietly. "So if anybody asks..."

Matty's eyes lit. "I get you," he said. "You never said nothing. Loose lips sink ships." He curled his finger and sealed his own mouth shut.

Kitty smiled. "I knew I could count on you."

"Will you bring him back to us, Aunt Kitty?"

"I don't know if I can."

"Well. Here. If you find him, give him the Lou Gehrig card. Maybe he didn't mean to leave it here."

"I'm sure he didn't."

"Do you think the Yankees will ever make it into another World Series without Lou, Aunt Kitty?"

She touched the top of Matty's head. "They'd better," she said quietly, "The Iron Horse is counting on them."

* * *

After a habitual check of the ways to get out, Luke finished eating his friend's gift peach and took his place at Isaiah Morgenstern's back room.

Those sitting around the table were an odd assortment. They were male except for Isabelle Marius, young, except for Isaiah, their middle-years host, and the gray-bearded Baram Gershom, whose ancient eyes were intelligent and curious. Each was scented, like Isaiah was, with his craft. Baram smelled of his offering, the beeswax candles that lit the room in the gathering twilight. Around Alain and Isabelle Marius swarmed the dark red richness of the product of their wine cellars. In the middle of the table stemmed glasses circled two long-necked green bottles. Beautiful Isabelle somehow secreted gunpowder under her floral perfume.

Luke supposed he was scented like Reuben Altshul's profession, thanks to that man's quick and expert replacing of his light colored suit with a dark one that would make Luke blend in better here, in this Jewish village within the city of New York.

They gathered, not like the crew of renegade international agents they were, but like his relatives at home, about to plan a blessingway or kinaalda. Isabelle patted Luke's knee, smiling. He covered it with his own. Her hand was cold.

"So," Isaiah called them to order. "It's so good my ancient father found himself a new wife with a nice place in the Bronx and left the business to me.

The two of them don't have to know about how pitifully the books are running in red ink. Or in what unusual manner we keep the Sabbath. Before our ceremony together, my friends, what information have we gathered for the aid of our guest, the Captain? Alain?"

Luke listened closely to the French agent's voice. "My journalist contact, he says if there were no patrons at Rumplemeyer's, they were, perhaps, warned away."

"Pointing to?"

"What the newspapers suppose, that the attack was the rough justice of the crime underworld. The police are following that direction in their investigation. Eh bien, most of them are."

"Most of them?"

"The scum of the police department arrived on the scene first. This is disturbing, you see? Although it, too, may signal that they were on notice from the bosses of crime, my friend has reliable connections there, also. No leaks about an attack came his way, before or after. No one claiming credit for the killing of a very small time operator, not even the one recently released from jail. So, my friend, he thinks perhaps it was supposed to look like the gangsters."

"Their aim was not a sham, not if they made a kill," Baram observed.

"Glass killed the one who welcomed us in," Luke said softly. "Opened the artery in his neck. He was not targeted, I think."

Alain Marius gave out a low whistle. "Were they aiming for you, Luke?"

"I'm not sure."

Isaiah frowned. "All right, let's leave that to stew," he suggested, before turning his attention to Alain's wife.

Luke remembered Isabelle Marius as a fearless woman who had landed an airplane with her wounded husband unconscious at her feet.

"Isabelle, my dear, did you find anything about this Nolan?" Isaiah asked. "Luke says this beat cop is abusing children of the republic! He sounds like the SS."

Isabelle nodded. "This Sergeant Nolan, he has a reputation for doing that, without regard to his ideology. We found something interesting, however. He was a great admirer of Charles Lindberg." She said the aviator's name the way Luke's sisters' spoke of the men who tried to cheat them at the trading post.

"Isolationist? How could Isolationists know about Luke?"

"Only that he is a valuable agent," Alain speculated. "One who caused diplomatic catastrophe when he unlocked one of Franco's worst prisons. Perhaps that is enough, yes?"

"An O.S.S. secret weapon, who is dangerous to Isolationist, Fifth column, betrayal-from-within plans?" Reuben Altshul suggested, eying Luke more closely. "Is that who you are, my long-sized comrade?"

Isabelle smiled wide. "Our angel of light is as prized as that? Well then, why not?"

Isaiah Morgenstern nodded. "The Americans are hoping to achieve some victories through this project Luke is working on, I think?"

"And more home front support for the war effort would be the result," Isabelle claimed.

"A blow for the remaining Isolationists," her husband concluded before Luke could protest that he did not think he was nearly so important.

"Exactly!" Isabelle proclaimed. "Or, perhaps it was more personal, yes? That is what I have found in my path of study, gentlemen. This Nolan has had past differences with the husband and brother of Madame Charente, both, no?"

Luke felt his fears for Kitty and her family returning. The Frenchwoman's arched brow lowered. "You do not know of this, Luke?" she asked.

"Husband and brother?"

"Her brother had a dispute with the mayor's relative, some years ago," she explained quietly. "Her husband and our Jack Spenser intervened with authorities of the city hall. The result? Detective Nolan becomes demoted to Sergeant again for his part in the affair."

Luke remembered his desire to take Nolan down. The darkness did not come from the blue coat, but from the one inside it. He suddenly needed to assure himself that Kitty was well. She had suffered enough since they'd met. Perhaps, later, in the darkness, he could go back. He felt Isaiah Morgenstern's hand at his shoulder.

"So, my bunkie," he said, "we have managed to come up with a number of possible sources of your less-than-welcoming first day in my city. Any more you care to add?"

"The O.S.S.," Luke said quietly.

Silence, broken by the gentle candle maker's voice. "Why, son? When they have trained you, worked so hard on this secret project of yours?"

"That is why," Luke unleashed his fear. "They believe in the ... project. In the wrong hands, there's no hope for it ever working. If they think anything was compromised, if they do not trust my word that I did not, would not give the beginnings of the project to the enemy, then I am a necessary casualty. Better to scrap me than the program."

The room grew cooler in the silence.

Alain Marius steepled his fingers under his chin. "Our friend has grown more worldly wise than when last we met, I think."

Isaiah Morgenstern smiled sadly. "And we have been answering questions with questions. But I hope our investigations will prove useful."

Isaiah then placed a black-paged scrapbook and a late edition of The New York Times on the table. "Let us now include my honored guest in our weekly ceremony. So he knows he is among friends here, at least."

All nodded agreement.

The watchmaker opened the newspaper's first section with spare precision until he found the page he wanted, and began to read aloud.

He had a fine voice, a good singer's voice. Luke had told him that once, in prison. Isaiah Morgenstern had laughed, said he wouldn't be mistaken for a holy man by his watchmaker father, angry at him for enlisting in the Lincoln Brigade in the Spanish Civil War.

Now, around this table, Isaiah Morgenstern read like a holy man, with reverence, and deep sadness. Luke concentrated on his friend's voice, on how the words were read, because the story was almost beyond his comprehension.

They all listened intently to the short article about great numbers of slaughtered people.

Baram placed his fisted hand to his heart once, twice, three times. Luke's mouth went dry. He tried to savor again taste of the last of his peach's sweetness, for all those in the story, who could not.

Then Isaiah Morgenstern methodically cut out the section of the newspaper, handed it to Baram, who opened the paste jar. The scrapbook was full of such clippings. It took in a new artifact.

This was a ritual, like those of his people, Luke thought again. In this small place without windows, with only the candles and gleaming bottles of French wine, a ritual.

"What page of the newspaper was the story on this time?" Baram asked, his voice heavy with sorrow.

"Sixteen," Isaiah said. "Beside the water main break on Sixth Avenue, and the advertisement of a sale on shoes at Gimbels. That's where they put report of the massacre, in Russia, of twenty thousand men, women, children. Perhaps we should cut out the whole page, my friends, so all in the future can see that the slaughter of our people sat beside a sale on shoes?"

Isaiah's ironic smile faded as he turned to Luke. "There are two wars being fought by Germany. One against the Allies. The other against the Jews, the gypsies, homosexuals, discontents. The first is everywhere. The other is buried. On page eight, sixteen, twenty-four."

Isabelle Marius shrugged. "What do you expect from the New York Times?"

"Better. I expect much better. From the newspaper of Ochs and Sulzberger," Isaiah countered, his face flush with indignation.

"Mais bien sur," Alain Marius took up his wife's argument, "It is a newspaper owned by Jews, edited by Catholics, for readers who are Protestants. And the Protestants, they want to read about tennis matches, not massacres. They do not want to fight a war to save outsiders, to save Jews."

"Neither does Roosevelt," Isaiah Morgenstern conceded. "Remember when they called the New Deal the "Jew" deal? What did he do? Ran the other way. He won't help now."

"I still say silent diplomacy..." Baram began.

"Silence is the enemy!" Isaiah disagreed. "Now, just as it was when Henry Ford published the Protocols of Zion. We should have lifted our voices together at that slanderous lie then, and again after Kristallnacht. Look, peacemaker, I'm not saying America is a bad country. It's the hope of the world. But these people with their blessed liberty, they have not seen what we have, my friend. Ah, wait. You should excuse me, please, for some have," he corrected himself, his calm eyes capturing Luke's. "Before the pogroms brought us to these shores, America's African slaves were not blessed by liberty. Neither were the people of our friend, Captain Kayenta, who even so would not betray his country or leave that prison without me, an American who he had no orders to save. Our captain, he will remember this testimony with which we end our very secular Shabbat."

As he said the words, Luke recalled the Dinè Council members offering conflicting advice about his own entry into the service. The Americans will not keep their promises, some said. When have they ever kept promises to us, these belegaanas with their eternal thirst for war? But Luke had become their warrior, and now he had to help them against such men as the Nazis, who would destroy a people.

"What can we do to get the attention of the press, while there are any of our relatives left?" Isaiah breathed out softly over his assembly.

Luke closed his eyes, asking his yei, holy people, for guidance. "Call yourselves something else," he said.

"What? Not Jews?"

Luke opened his eyes. Story. Explain with story. "When the Dinè were in our exile, after the Long Walk, our forced migration, we were dying of hunger and sickness," he began. "My grandmother, who was a young girl then, she told me the story. We needed to return to our own land, that we knew, that knew us, you see? We stopped calling ourselves Dinè, or their word for us: Navajo. Those Navajo, they made war with the federal soldiers. They were unfit for liberty that the real Americans had as birthright. So we called ourselves farmers and shepherds, who only wanted a chance to return to the mountains and canyons of home."

Baram locked sad eyes on Luke. "And it worked? Did you return home, my friend?"

"We did."

"So, your tribe also lived in exile, like ours did, in Egypt. But our people, now, in this time, what do we call ourselves, dear shepherd? Who are we?"

"Those fleeing the ravages of this war," Luke said. "The same as the people -- the suffering ones they put on the front pages of their newspapers, who have faces that look like themselves. What is the word?" He scanned the newspaper. "Here it is: 'refugees.'"

From inside the watchmaker's shop, the parrot Ezechiel squawked.

"Strange," Isaiah, said, rising. "Please, my friends, sit tight. And quietly." He walked toward the curtained window.

They waited. Heard low voices. Luke reached inside his vest, to his shoulder holster. He rose, ready. But Isaiah returned through the curtain, and he was smiling. "A young goy woman talented with hairpins in a locked door but not so good with birds would like to speak with you, Luke," he said

Chapter 11

Kitty folded her arms, surveying his form, trying to hide her crazy delight over finding him. "The Prince Albert suit's right, but without a beard or side curls, I don't think you'll pass as Hasidic."

Luke glanced back at where the small man was disappearing behind the clock shop's curtained doorway before he dead-sighted her.

"What are you doing here?"

Angry. He was angry? "You could say hello, considering my home's been trashed for your sake."

He grabbed her arms, made her eyes meet his. His voice quieted. "Kitty. Not only your home."

She glanced away.

He eased his grip, but brought her closer, close enough that she could see tailor's chalk marks on the lapel of his new suit jacket, and smell that he'd been eating fruit, summer fruit. Peaches.

"Are you well now, Kitty?" he asked in that soft drawl.

She twisted for a measure of freedom. "Sure, I'm all right."

He released her, seeing something else, she knew it -- her disappointment in the loss of even his rough hold. How else did that shy sheepherder gather up enough courage to swoop down and kiss her? Peach-flavored kisses. The clocks' ticking around them intensified, or was it his pulse she heard, keeping its own time, as his hands circled her waist? He breathed against her throat.

"How did you come here?"

She opened her eyes, saw the fingers of her left hand stroking the hard, wide plane of his face. Her marriage band and engagement diamond glinted back at her as she found her voice. "Subway, with two connections more than I had to, just in case. Nobody knows the subways like I do. I'm alone, don't worry."

"Good."

Approval. Yes, she realized, she needed that, after Jack's exasperation, after Dr. Saltzman's contempt. Kitty needed Luke's approval, as much as she needed the sweet, seductive breath that swept across the curve of her face.

"But you should not be here," he still insisted.

"I could say the same for you, Captain."

"I'm on furlough."

"Oh?" she managed to breath out as he kissed down the path she made by unbuttoning her best crepe-de-chine blouse.

"Yes. Information gathering." His nose guided the strap of her slip off her shoulder.

"With anarchists? Communists?" she challenged.

"The O.S.S. sometimes makes unconventional friends."

"I've noticed."

The texture of his hair surprised her, it was like fluid silk, escaping between her fingers even as she fisted it.

He came up for air, his eyes dazed, boyish. "How do your ear ornaments stay on?"

"On?"

"Without the skin being pierced."

"You're trying to distract me." Trying? He had her primed to go down with him behind the grandfather clock.

"Kitty," he whispered. "Take them off."

"Off?"

"The ornaments. Your ears are so beautiful."

Her fingers found the clips behind the gold toned metal, the aurora borealis rhinestones. She released them, pulled. Slowly, enjoying the sparks in the eyes she thought were solid black. His tongue traced the contours of her ears then, a dizzying reward. Her head fell back as he kissed down her neck and between, inside the thin cotton of her bandeau bra then around the bared curve of each breast. The teasing feel of his erection at her middle was all it took to send her over the edge. She'd never before come with a man still outside her. With her hat still on.

He groaned softly, stepping back from their embrace. His hand returned her silk slip's straps over her shoulder. He buttoned her blouse slowly, carefully, kissing her steaming cheeks.

"Thank you. For all you've done, suffered. But you must go now."

Dismissed? He was not her superior, but her prey. Think again, shepherd. "Not without you."

"Mr. Spenser wants to lock me away."

"No. He's on your side, Luke. He's fighting for you."

"Against whom? The ones who already think I have cracked?"

"I don't know. Aw, Luke, I'm new at this job."

He laughed. A hollow sound, but not without humor. His hand cupped the side of her face. "I will stay here with my friend a little while, where I can breathe, where I can learn things of value."

She leaned her cheek into his hold. "Don't you think Jack knows who your friends are?"

He blinked. "Did you tell him?"

"No. Neither did Matty, not that they bothered to ask him."

"But you did talk with Matty. That's how you found me."

"Yes."

He smiled. Approval again, perhaps admiration. Why did she need it?

The small, bald man who'd first ushered her into the shop now burst in from the back. His eyes lit when he found them. "Here, here, then, my love-bird customers!" he proclaimed.

Kitty adjusted her off-kilter hat, then looked up to see Luke's eyes boring into someone else; a man dressed in a long, belted raincoat and standing in the curtained doorway.

The proprietor hurried forward, shoving something into Luke's hand. "The watch is all repaired, running good again!" He turned them both toward the shop's front door. "I'll take nothing for the fix, if you don't tell my neighbors that the unobservant schmendrick Morgenstern opened up the shop for you before sundown," he said.

A low growl broke from Luke's throat.

"Thank you, Mr. Morgenstern," Kitty said.

"There, now! Someone has good manners! Mazel Tov. Go, go, round back, round back home, now, young ones. Fly away home, lovebirds."

The parrot began an unearthly shriek.

The watchmaker tried to laugh. "Ezechiel, you old nuisance! So orthodox!" He pushed them down the aisle, unlocked and opened the front door. "Go, go, so I can calm him down."

He closed and locked the door behind them, then pulled down its blackout shade.

Kitty frowned. "Well! Your Mr. Morgenstern was in a hurry to..." she began, until silenced by Luke's iron grip on her hand.

"Come."

"Where?"

"Where he said."

"Said?"

"Around back."

He led her into the alley, to a space that jutted out the back of the tenement building, one story high, with one door.

Luke scanned the alley. "No sentries. They are over-sure of themselves," he whispered.

"Who?"

He motioned her silent, then found two wooden crates and set them down beside the brick wall.

Kitty steadied the crates as he climbed to the flat roof and its skylight. Luke offered his hand and hauled her up behind him.

The squares of wired glass were grimy but they could see the candlelit figures in the room below.

Kitty tried to make sense of the scene: an oblong table, people sitting around it, very still. Isaiah Morgenstern entered, followed closely by the man in the raincoat.

The raincoat man spoke, but Kitty couldn't understand the words. Three men dressed like him stood behind those who were seated: three men and a woman. It looked like a children's game to her, like Duck, Duck, Goose or A Tisket, A Tasket. One of the seated men had his head down on the table as if he'd fallen asleep. A pool of red was growing under it, seeping into the pages of an opened scrapbook. The man standing behind him held up a thin wire taut between gloved hands.

How strange, raincoats and gloves in summer, Kitty thought.

The man moved on to the woman's chair. A beautiful woman, staring stoically forward. My God. He's going to kill her too, Kitty thought, pressing her hand to her mouth.

"Give me your rings," Luke said.

"My—?"

He slipped the bands from her finger. Her wedding ring jerked into the air, hit the drainpipe, landed on the old cobblestones. Luke fisted her diamond engagement ring. The rain coated man's voice rose in pitch and intensity. Luke carved a crude circle in the glass pane. Someone inside laughed.

"Your shoe, Kitty," Luke implored, desperation edging his voice.

She slipped one of her high heels off, put it into his palm. His hand braced on her shoulder. He pushed, sending her a full arm's length from him.

"Stay," he whispered.

She nodded.

Inside, the game continued. Upon a gruff command, the standing men shifted around the table. Each snapped his thin wire taut as they leaned over the heads of the remaining seated. Their hands were tied behind their backs. One of the men was dead, and the rest and the beautiful woman were about to be executed. And the watchmaker was being forced to watch, helpless.

It all came together.

Luke tapped Kitty's red shoe's heel against the glass. It broke with a chink, a small sound. The leader detected it, she thought, for his raised hand hesitated.

His men reached into their coats. Flashes of metal. Guns. Kitty felt Luke exhale. Then, a shot, through the hole he's made in the glass. Below, one face registered mild surprise. The rain coated man collapsed, even as the muzzle of his gun shifted from the watchmaker's back to them, beyond the skylight. He fired.

Its glass shattered, making a large opening.

Luke calmly shifted position. He passed his gun to his left hand and released a shot. It brought down the second gunman.

Luke had told her he was ambidextrous. Was he that way naturally or did he work at it, Kitty wondered.

Isaiah Morgenstern wheeled around, flinging a blue bowl, which knocked another exploding gun off course. Peaches tumbled to the floor.

Three more shots, from Luke's right hand this time. Then, smoke. And silence.

Luke crawled across the splintered glass and twisted wire of the skylight. He returned her shoe.

"I dropped your ring. I'm sorry."

"That's all right."

"Bunkie?" Isaiah Morgenstern called from below.

Luke waved to the man inside the room, now smelling of smoke and blood. Then he scuttled across the roof and swung down easily. He gave Kitty his hand, steadying her until she reached the ground.

The watchmaker Morgenstern slipped out the back door. The woman followed, took Luke's head between her hands, pressed their foreheads together.

"Well done, Ange de Lumière," she said, kissed him on one side of his face, then the other.

"Alain sends his thanks, also. He makes things ready for the police, as best he can."

The woman handed blood-stained documents to Morgenstern.

"Swiss passports, false," the watchmaker reported, handing them to Luke. "Recognize any?"

Luke opened the passports, looked at the small photographs. "No, sir." He returned the documents to the watchmaker.

"They used German Lugers."

"Is Baram...?"

"Yes, dead, before any of us could do a thing. Peace be with our peacemaker."

"Sergeant Morgenstern, did I...?"

"Bring them here? No, my friend. Their leader was very proudly boasting that an informer, a no-good dirty beat cop, told them of our newspaper clipping service meetings. A simple, quiet way to finish us off together, that was the plan, once I got rid of the young couple, the customers in my shop, right? They allowed this. That was their mistake. These pishers, they like to brag, terrorize first. It gave you time to find a position above us. Well done, my bunkie, and your lady."

"So," the Frenchwoman said. "One of ours, four of theirs are down. Our salvation bears your earmarks, my Ange. The ones who sent them down upon us, they may also surmise that you were here, eh? So may your own people. Except for this one," she smiled at Kitty after a quick assessment, "who chooses good men, and who I think will not betray you."

In the distance, a police siren sounded.

"Go, now," Mr. Morgenstern urged. "We'll take care of things here. Remember that you have friends, Captain, and..."

"Madame Charante," the Frenchwoman said.

Isaiah Morgenstern eyes softened. "Of course. Madame Charante." He took Kitty's hand and cradled it between his own. "I am so happy we have finally met. But for now, the both of you, go with God."

The Frenchwoman and the watchmaker returned to the back room, closing the door behind them.

Luke strapped his gun back into his holster. His face was smeared with the lipstick of two women. He was scented with gunpowder from what he'd done— calmly, mechanically killed four men with five shots.

"Kitty," he breathed out. "You should leave now."

"Nothing doing, Shepherd," she said. "You're with me. Where do we go?"

He sighed hard. "Where we can disappear. Somewhere crowded."

Kitty took his hand, which was shaking badly.

Chapter 12

Luke never thought riding on iron rails beneath a teeming city could be soothing, but it was. It was as if the chindi of those four men could never find him here, with one hand clutching his jish bag, the other in the firm grip of the airman's wife.

Kitty. Her name is Kitty. Katherine. Give her, her name, it is not forbidden, not taboo, because she is alive. Perhaps it would help keep her alive, if he thought of her by name. Because she seemed determined to stay beside him, as dangerous as that had proved to be.

"Now do you need a stiff drink?" she asked.
"No. Alcohol is like the cow's milk with me."
"Allergic?"
"Mostly, yes."
"Well. What do you need?"
"Anaaji," he said, without thinking.
"What's that?"
"It is a ceremony. Called, in the English, Enemy Way. It takes a long time, five nights, with much singing and ritual. By its end I might frighten you, dressed as Monster Slayer, blackened with tallow and ashes."

"You wouldn't frighten me."

"No?"

"No."

Luke smiled, touching the side of her face, as he would in ceremony, with corn pollen to protect her. "Then maybe you would sing the songs of Changing Woman, helping to put things back into proper places, restore beauty."

No, that was wrong. Kitty was a foreigner, not even allowed into the ceremony. She would never be asked to take part. He had spoken out of his loneliness. But she was smiling, so he could not find the heart to tell her his mistake.

"Tell me the name again," she said.

"Anaaji."

She repeated the word in his language, her life breath warming his chin, mingling with his, spreading like love medicine. Had he sent out medicine with the name, to capture this foreign woman and her large doe eyes?

He was sorry for the things she had seen. But she had a warrior's heart. It was all right to give her this gift: a word from his language. He doubted it ever would be a code word, for it was about spirit life, not tanks and bombs and military strategy.

The belegaanas were always trying to change the religion of the Dinè, because it was so different from their own. But this woman asked to hear the sound of his language. Then she gave the word her strength, honored it. How could he tell her that? And how much it pleased him.

"How did the French woman know my name?"

"She was acquainted with your husband."

"Oh."

"Not in that way, Kitty. On missions. Isabelle is very charming, she likes men and all the men love her. But she is devoted to her husband. His is in service too."

"Alain. The one who makes things ready for police inspection."

"Yes."

"I see."

But Luke was not sure she believed him. "Your husband, he was always showing us photographs of you, of your family."

"Did he?"

"Yes. Of course. You lived in his heart."

She was quiet for so long he feared he had said too much. Or too little. Then she squeezed his hand. "Say, Shepherd, do you dance?" she asked him.

"Yes," he said.

The doe eyes narrowed at his quick response. "The new dances?"

"Charleston?"

"The Charleston's the Lindy Hop now, except it doesn't hop any more, it sort of pumps along, and is called the jitterbug."

"Show me. I will learn. And I can show you the fandango."

She smiled. "You're on."

"On? On what?"

"I mean we agree, rube."

"Rube. This is something your nephew calls me too. What does it mean, Kitty?"

"That you're a country boy."

"Well, that's true, I am."

"In spades."

"Spades?"

She rolled her eyes, making him laugh.

"Where are we going Kitty?"

"Uptown."

"Past Spenser's building?"

"Much past Spenser. To a dance hall called the Savoy. It will be crowded, so we can disappear for a little while. And nobody asks questions at the Savoy. About who you are, where you come from. Who you dance with. Even what color you are."

"I see."

She sat back in the rocking seat. "I'd sure like to change my clothes."

"Jack will have someone watching your place."

"I know. Hey, Alice lives right off this line. We can stop at her apartment first, so I can change."

"Alice?"

"Who waited on us yesterday at the Westminster? Bossy? Good legs?"

"Yes. Alice."

"I'll borrow something of hers. And I can telephone Mama from there, tell her that we're all right. She'll be worried."

"We can't have her worry."

Kitty narrowed her eyes again. "Hey. Are you making fun of me? The O.S.S. operative who has to call home?"

He held his hands palms up. "No. Mothers are powerful. I would not want to offend any. Especially one who looks like the shining woman in the harbor."

"You're not exactly the cloak and dagger spy type yourself, you know."

"Yes. I know."

"I'll bet you'd rather be bedding down your sheep right now."

"If you were there," he said quietly. And the bed he saw in his mind's eye was hers.

She squeezed his hand again. It filled him with pleasure, but he didn't look at her. She would see his thoughts. She would laugh. With belegaana women love medicine was not the same. He had learned that. But it was so hard to remember, with this one.

"Luke, why are your hands still soft, soft enough for Pop to know you worked with sheep?"

"After the prison, I was ... damaged."

She nodded, listening. Listening deeply, he sensed.

"They flew me into a hospital in Scotland. It was in the countryside. I was getting better at shearing time. Sheep stations always need help at shearing time. So I slipped over the wall."

"You escaped your hospital?"

"Well, yes."

She laughed like a child laughs, free and bubbling up, like a spring.

"It was only a short wall."

Her laughter rose in pitch. She had so much life. How could the airman love the skies more than this woman? She anchored her hand at his shoulder. "It's a good thing you're in the O.S.S., Luke. Only this branch of the service would put up with an agent who goes AWOL to shear sheep."

"Am I theirs any longer?"

"What do you mean?"

"I'm over the wall again, Kitty."

"With me. That makes a difference. We're just having a wilder weekend than planned. I'll see you home, just as I promised Jack."

"When?"

"When you're convinced that we're not your enemy."

"I like this way you see it."

She frowned. "You should try it sometime. Come on. This is our stop."

As he surveyed the subway's stairs, the street, then the structure, Luke didn't like the building where Kitty's friend lived. There were even monsters carved in stone over the high front doors. Stopping him cold. Kitty wove her arm through his.

"Just a few minutes," she said softly.

What reason could he give to deny those eyes? But he had work of his own to do. Kitty Charente, who was making him a woman's man again, he had to get away from her. Soon. But for now, he followed her up the iron stairway.

* * *

"Gosh, what happened to you?" Kitty demanded as her friend peered over the chain between her door and its frame.

Alice's fingers quickly danced along the mean red and purple swelling under her eye. "Soup pot at work. Burned myself good, huh?" She looked beyond Kitty. "Luke's with you?"

"Yes, he's right here, see? Wow, you need to take care of that eye, it's swollen shut! Say, Alice?

Do you think I might borrow a dress and use your phone?"

"Borrow...?"

"Yeah. I'm wearing my sister's skirt. I don't want Anya knowing the size of this stain before I can get it soaked and she's none the wiser. Want to help me out?"

"Well, sure, kiddo. Say, I'm glad to see ya both."

"Glad enough to let us in?"

"Oh, oh, sure. But hold on a minute."

The door closed. From inside came the scurrying sounds of footsteps and clinking glasses. Kitty looked up at Luke in the dim hall light. His eyes darted around the hallway.

"We should go, maybe," he said.

"This won't take long, I promise."

The door opened. Alice was in a silk dressing gown kimono, the kind that had suddenly gone out of fashion after Pearl Harbor. She'd thrown a sheer scarf over her living room's only lamp, so its collection of mahogany veneered furniture looked even darker. Alice inspected Kitty's skirt.

"Wow. Playing in the junkyard?"

"Well, Luke wanted to see all the sights."

"The Berry's attract trouble. Your Mr. Spenser should have found him an old boring chum like me. Sit down! Hey, I'm sorry about Rumplemeyers, Luke. You deserved a healthier welcome to New York. Jack Spenser buy you that spiffy new suit? I'd ask for a raise too, if I was you." She walked past them and into the bar set-up just inside her tiny kitchen. "Hey, what can I get you two?"

"The telephone for me, and a ginger ale for Luke," Kitty answered for them.

Once she'd called her mother and gotten Luke settled on the couch, Kitty welcomed the chance to back Alice into the apartment's bedroom.

Even there, her friend whirled about like she was the only waitress on at noon, yanking through the hangers in her closet with savage force.

"Going dancing?"

"Yeah."

"Where? Roseland?"

"I thought... well, I'm not sure."

"This lavender satin number would be best, I think, with Luke's new suit. I wonder if there's anything doesn't hang nice on that man. He's tall, you want to be able to move easily around his feet. This dress has got plenty of skirt, see?"

"Alice, will you look at me?"

Her friend's high-pitched laugh set Kitty's nerves on edge.

"What?"

"You've been looking over our heads, or around your rooms, like we're going to make off with the silver. And that's another thing. You're as neat as a pin, Alice. I've never seen this place anything but spotless before."

"Well." The side of her friend's mouth slackened. "You ain't been by lately, have you?"

That was true, Kitty realized. Since Philippe's death her life had revolved around work, family, and her solitude.

Alice's big bed was unmade. A picture of the seashore had its glass broken and was hanging crooked. And a pair of men's oxfords were under a chair by the window. Kitty took a deep breath and spoke slowly.

"Alice, you never burned yourself the whole time we were at the restaurant together."

"So? I'm on a lot of extra hours. We're short-handed."

Kitty came closer. "That's not a burn, it's a bruise. What's going on?"

Her friend's head cocked sideways. "You know how it is, at first with them. They've got to show you who's boss. Before they calm down. He'll calm down. Oh, come on, don't tell me Philippe never took a swing at you."

"He didn't," Kitty said quietly. "Not even in fun." Neither would Luke, the thought came, unbidden. Why wasn't her street-smart friend as lucky with men? "Alice, this guy. He's not worth it. He's dangerous. This is your place. You've got to throw him out."

"No. I got to get very drunk. And forget that you were here."

"What?"

Alice sank into the bed's springs. "Try on my lavender dress, will ya, Kitty? You can have it, I'm tired of the rag. I bet it will look swell."

Chapter 13

"Your friend has troubles," Luke said quietly as they walked back to the subway station.

"Yes. And she wouldn't spill them. I couldn't help her."

"She is on her own path, Kitty."

"And I have a stray keeping me busy enough for now."

He smiled. "You look very beautiful to me. I wanted to tell you that. When you showed me this dress."

"Oh? Why didn't you?"

"My breath was robbed by my eyes."

She stopped under the lamp post at the subway station. "Luke."

"Yes?"

"What a lovely thing to say."

"But I didn't say anything. That's what I'm trying to explain."

She shook her head as they descended the stairs. "You stood up when I came into the room. That was enough to impress Alice."

"Kitty, did you tell her where we were going?"

"No. She asked. I told her we hadn't decided. I'm getting good at this spy stuff, huh?"

He grinned, showing those beautiful teeth.

It was an in-between time of night, before the theaters let out, so the A train was not crowded. They even found an empty car. Once seated, Luke stared ahead.

Kitty had seen him go into his own thoughts before, but this was different. There was tension around his mouth. Of course. He was on watch, guarding them.

She slipped her arms around his damaged middle. His finger grazed her cheek, before his lips pressed the spot where Nolan had yanked hair from her scalp. Spreading warmth, healing.

"Luke, the Savoy Ballroom, it's sort of got a reputation, because it's so free."

"Free?"

"Open. For all kinds. What I'm saying is... we're going way uptown now, to Harlem. A colored neighborhood."

"Colored?"

"Negroes."

He nodded. "Black white people."

Laughter bubbled out of her. "What?"

"It's what my grandmother says, from when she first saw a Negro soldier, long ago, when she was a little girl. They were just like the belegaana, the white people, to her, wearing the same uniform, speaking English. So she called them black white people."

"Well, it's different here. At Rose Land, another dance club, they put up a rope, to separate black from white dancers. But the Savoy is a place where white and colored can dance together, without being bothered."

"Bothered?"

"Yes, you know, harassed. For, umm... for mixing." Please don't make him ask what that meant, she prayed, because all the other words were worse. The familiar confusion on his face was replaced by a grim understanding.

"What are you asking me?" he asked quietly.

"I just don't know how you feel about..."

"About being among black white people?"

"Well, yes."

"Kitty, I have been treated as less than human, as a savage by white people all my life. And my skin is dark. So this Savoy, this is a safe place for us to dance together, yes?"

"Well," she realized, "we won't stand out."

"Would we be harassed, even in this city where the world walks, if I were Spanish, or a Mexican?"

"Oh, some low life would figure out some reason it wasn't proper, sure."

"A low life? Like Nolan?"

She stared ahead. "Exactly like Nolan."

The train went around a curve, sending her closer against his side. Kitty stayed there, feeling his slow, even breathing. She looked up. He was on guard again. Why couldn't she see his eyes, Kitty wondered. Because he wasn't Philippe, closer to her height. He wasn't Philippe. And he didn't have to be. She tugged the sleeve of his black suit coat. "I want to dance with you, Luke."

He dead-sighted her then, as if she'd said something else, and maybe she had. He looked from her mouth to her eyes, asking her permission silently, beautifully, seductively. Kitty had always thought the old Valentino movies that Alice loved were silly, preferring the modern, wisecracking humor of Cary Grant and Clark Gable. Or Philippe Charente. But this man said so much in his spare words, his silences, his potent waiting. Could he see how charged she was getting, locked by those eyes, the smooth planes of his face, the wildness of his scent?

Those gentle hands circled her waist. They lifted her into his lap. He waited in the clacking rhythm of the empty train car. Waited for her nod. She gave it. His mouth descended on hers. Once. Again. Then hands. Strong soft, shepherd's hands, gliding past her knee. Higher.

"This pleases you?" he asked.

Kitty dragged her fingers down from his hair to straighten the knot of his tie. "It robs my breath."

She traced his upper lip with her tongue, delighting in the hum coming out of him, echoing the trains. "But if we don't—yes, there... stop... no, once more, yes, there. Oh, Luke... we're gonna end up in the Bronx."

"The fifth borough of New York City. The only one connected to the mainland of the United States," he recited, breathlessly, from that damned guidebook in his head, while his mouth and hands were going to other places entirely.

* * *

The cavernous room took up most of the second floor of a large building. It was painted the color of the pink sunsets over the towering canyons of home. Luke felt taken in, accepted, despite all the mirrors, which made him nervous, unsure of depth, of what was there, and what was reflection. On the east wall were two orchestras, one large and one smaller. One playing, and the other ready to take over, so that the music and dancing was continuous. And the dancers were not black and white, as Kitty had said, but people of all shades of color. The wooden floor seemed as much alive as the dancers, pulsing with the beat of the music. They moved, not in lines or circles like the dancers at home, but with his people's familiar exuberance.

Luke turned his attention back to their small table at the Savoy Ballroom, his heart full. He needed to give thanks for this place, this time. He took out his penknife and carefully sliced the paper off the cigarette from the pack he'd just bought. He emptied its tobacco in the clean ashtray, struck a match, set it on fire. Placing his hands over the small conflagration, he watched the white smoke seep through his fingers, rising steadily toward the colored lights of the ballroom. A good sign. He brushed a little of the smoke toward his face, inhaling. A Chesterfield cigarette did not contain sacred tobacco, but it would have to do.

"Hey! You trying to torch the joint?"

He looked up, baffled. The woman who had sold him the cigarettes, the one whose skin was the rich shade of coffee, smiled down on him. It was good then, whatever she had said.

She placed two bubbling drinks on the table. "Your girl powdering her nose?"

"Yes." That's what Kitty had said, 'I'm going to powder my nose.' How do women know exactly what other women do in those rooms?

"Your change." Their waitress held out a bill and a handful of coins. He didn't need them. He had too much. And he was used to his women dealing with belegaana money.

"For you," he told their waitress.

"You mean it?"

"Sure." He liked that word: 'sure,' and the good feeling it seemed to inspire in people who heard it.

"Sharp new suit. Big spender. And he drinks soda pop besides? I hope your woman knows how to hold onto you."

"She does."

"You'll tell her that I offered you change, right? That I didn't take advantage of your good nature? That woman looked like she'd punch out anybody came near you."

"She might," he agreed.

The waitress laughed. "Well, thanks for the warning, I'm not looking for trouble. Hey, you enjoy your view, now, Boy Scout. Our Ella's making a special visit to the bandstand for a song tonight. You want to get closer, you look for me, hear? I'll slip you up."

"Thank you."

Another good sign, this woman, Luke thought, as she walked away.

The remaining white curls of smoke from his small ceremony rose through his vision of the dancers. He recognized some of their steps. He'd learned a few at school. And more at his training base in California. Kitty Charente wanted to dance with him, she had said so. And she would not laugh as her brothers beat him after the dance, like that other one.

"Luke. You smoke?"

Kitty appeared across from him. He hadn't heard her approach, hadn't had the pleasure of watching her long-legged stride, of holding her chair out for her. He'd been too lost in the music, the dancing. This was not good.

He passed the blunt Chesterfield pack over to her half of the table. "Kitty," he reminded her, "tobacco was one of our gifts to your people, remember?"

"Oh, jeepers. That's right." She laughed, her hand covering her mouth, her teeth, like a shy girl. Another part of her she was allowing him to see.

Kitty picked up the pack, knocked it against the side of her hand. Two cigarettes flew out, landing in her lap. Her smile turned crooked.

"Quite the sophisticate, huh?"

Luke suspected that she smoked about as often as he did. "The Dinè don't know about sophistication," he said. "For us, tobacco is sacred. For ceremony."

She gave him that sideways look. "We don't have to climb up eighty-six stories for another ceremony now do we, ya big ape?"

He laughed, so grateful to her for easing the burdens of the past terrible hours. Terrible and wonderful, he realized as he flicked the match to flame and held it to her cigarette, then his. The look in her eyes made the crowded room slip away. He sat back and drew the tobacco's smoke into his lungs, burning into his memory the steady rock of the subway train, the feel of her thigh in the hold of his hand. That memory. Not his kills. Or the brutal prison guard holding their burning iron rod against his flesh. Go away from there. Go toward Kitty, and this place with its welcome.

As the dance ended, a woman dressed in sky blue stood on the bandstand. Everyone hushed for her song.

"Looking everywhere, haven't found him yet," she half-sung and half-storied, "He's the big affair I cannot forget..." The singer's eyes were deep as a canyon pool after a rain. Her plaintive voice called herself the lamb looking for her shepherd. Her song filled him with longing for home.

Luke watched Kitty through the ribbons of smoke between them, remembering the story a grandmother at Babbitt's trading post had told him once, when he was a child. In the story Coyote created the races of the world's people from clay. The ones he pulled out of the kiln first were the white people, then the yellow, then the red, and last the black. He and Kitty Charente and the woman with the beautiful voice and all the dancers were like those in the Coyote story. The same, only out of different batches. This place was the kiln.

"Oh how I need someone to watch over me," the woman finished her song. She smiled shyly, and left the bandstand's stage while the room still rocked with applause.

"She is a singer," Luke said.

Kitty laughed. "And then some! The Duke's got a duchess of song."

"No, I mean..." How could he explain it? "My people would say she has medicine, a calling, a gift."

Kitty reached across their table, tracing his knuckles with the pads of her fingers. "Yes. I understand. I agree."

He extinguished the cigarette in the ashes of his small ceremony as the band began playing again. "Let's dance." He captured her hand.

* * *

Kitty caught her breath after One O'clock Jump, grateful that it was a tune she and Philippe had never danced to. "Why, Luke, you can cut a rug!"

His puzzled look dissolved into a wide grin. "You follow, complete the dance. You make it beautiful."

The band's leader tapped the musicians into a slower rhythm for You Made Me Love You. Luke winced, then cast a glance toward their table.

"You're not getting away from me yet," Kitty warned him. The low lights dimmed further. They fell into the slower step easily as the singer took up the old tune. Kitty could hear his heartbeat, still hammering fast. She stepped back.

There was pain there, on his face. Heartache. She was not the only one with the memory of dancing with another, she realized. And to this song. But he was not sad with longing. This past lover. She had hurt him.

Kitty swept her thumb across his wide palm. "Hey, Shepherd. I'm not her," she whispered.

His grim expression softened. "No," he confirmed, pulling her again under his heart.

There. The beating steadied. How could any woman hurt this man, Kitty wondered, as she lost herself in the sultry music, and the warmth of Luke Kayenta's embrace.

"May I cut in?"

The voice triggered Luke's low, protective growl.

"Don't worry," the affable voice responded to it. "We're country cousins, Yank. And I'd be pleased enough to sit down and speak with you both, if you don't think our Kitty would be secure in my arms."

"Alec." Kitty knew the voice before she recognized the face. Her husband's squadron leader had grown a thin red mustache since the funeral, when she'd screamed at him for not keeping Philippe safe.

"Alexander Fitzgibbon," he finished introducing himself to Luke. "Now of the Royal Canadian Corps of Signals. A great pleasure to meet you, Captain Kayenta."

Luke's scowl eased, but he still waited for Kitty's nod before they led Alexander Fitzgibbon to their table.

"How did you find us?" Kitty asked, once there.

"You two have a number of guardian angels. Quarreling with each other at present, about where you might be and what to do about your highly unofficial status." Alec looked around, smiled. But he lowered his voice so that the three of them leaned their heads toward the middle of the table.

"The Americans and British are running the show, as usual. Nobody speaks to us Corpsmen much, but Canadians aren't as dumb as we look, eh? Especially this one, who remembers favorite haunts well enough to check for you here." He leaned in closer, although no one could have heard them over the band's music, Kitty was sure. "Now," Alec continued, "you'd think your angels would deign to work better together since the elimination of some highly sought-after 'Swiss' nationals, eh?"

Kitty saw Luke's eyes grow hooded with careful indifference.

"Good work, Captain," Alec said, the humor replaced by admiration in his voice.

"Not assigned work," Luke stated bluntly.

Alec's eyebrows disappeared in the carefully dressed curls on his forehead. "No, you are quite right. And we are well aware that it could have had an uglier result. Three of our allied agents were guests among those around that table. We are in your debt, sir."

Luke's attention darted to the exits. His hands had disappeared from their sight, too, Kitty realized.

"Be at ease," Alec said. "There will be no squabbling amongst us over your action. Oh, except from Hoover, who wants bag-'em credit if any kills go public. Here's a rare point of agreement among us: we'll be glad to give it to him, after."

"After...?" Kitty prompted.

"After the capture of the rest of them, my love."

Kitty found Luke's hand as it slipped out of his vest. She held it fast. "Alec, who were those men in back of Mr. Morgenstern's shop?"

"Nazi saboteurs, left by U-boat off Nova Scotia, with false passports, supplies, currency. We Canadian agents have been after them since their arrival. They are more professional than those poor bastards that came in off Montauk and Florida. Slippery, better trained, this bunch. Recently our agents have been joined by the bloody English, the French Resistance and perhaps an old Cossack or two in pursuit.

"Now that they've crossed the border into the States, Donovan's O.S.S., Hoover's F.B.I. and Lord knows how many other of your president's alphabet soup of agencies are in the mix. The way we're tripping over one another, a sky full of Luftwaffe seems safer."

Their waitress appeared at Luke's side, frowning at Alec's arm bridging to Kitty's chair.

"What can I get you, sir?"

"Another round of ginger ales, please," Kitty ordered.

The waitress left only after Luke nodded. "How many more of the enemy are there?" he asked quietly.

"We're not sure," Alec admitted. "They've been operating in groups of two, three, four. Spreading down along our Canadian coast, hitting transportation, industry, power plants, even a department store. Using everything from bombs, to acids to exploding pencils."

"Why haven't we heard about this? In the papers? Over the radio?" Kitty asked.

"Oh, you've heard, my darling girl: about accidents, system failures, unsolved murders. Look, Kitty, the East and Western seaboards of both our countries are nervous enough. The Axis submarines have coastal shipping paralyzed here in the East. The public doesn't need to know the enemy has landed, and has Fifth Column help from those America First fanatics."

Kitty squeezed Luke's hand: calm, dry, warm, everything hers was not.

"Yes. They've had co-operation from the inside, I'm afraid," Alec continued. "We got that much from two we captured and hauled up to Ottawa. Captain Kayenta, you made the first kills, of the four about to wipe out Isaiah Morgenstern's stateside club of international rabble rousers. I imagine you're now quite the prize."

The waitress returned, placing their drinks on the table, accepting Alec Fitzgibbon's tip with a one-handed flip and catch. Her fist rested on Luke's shoulder, as her look squared on Kitty. "If you go with Red, send your leftovers my way, will you, honey?"

"Not even for dessert," Kitty warned.

Alec Fitzgibbon sighed deeply as he watched the waitress depart. "I'm the Van Johnson of the R.A.F. The best friend. Never destined to get the girl, eh?"

Suddenly, his eyes narrowed.

"Alec, what is it?" Kitty whispered.

"Nothing, darling. Perhaps we ought to keep up this love triangle scenario, however," he suggested as the band began a foxtrot. He stood. "Captain, another deep scowl if you please, while I steal your woman?"

Luke's hand went cold before it released hers. "It is Kitty's choice," he finally said.

She stood, not wanting to. Silly. The waitress wasn't going to abduct Luke. He'd be waiting.

Alec spun her toward the middle of the dance floor, pressing her close, his lips at her ear. "The Germans want him badly. Alive."

"Why?"

"That I don't know. Knowledge is power, and I'm merely the country cousin, remember? I suspect you know more than I." There was a bitter edge to his voice. "Kitty, does Jack suspect he's a double agent? Perhaps a taller-than-usual former Son of Heaven under that tan? Maybe a half-breed American Jap?"

"No!"

"Easy, darling. I'm wondering why the other side wants him breathing, after the damage he's done. He must have something the Nazis can get out of him. To give, as a gift, to keep Japan in the war with them, perhaps? 'A prized timepiece,' Jack called him. How does Luke Kayenta seem to you, Kitty? At least one of Jack's consultants think he's already popped a spring."

"Saltzman."

"Dr. Saltzman, exactly."

"They've never even met."

"Much to the good doctor's consternation. You're not of the same opinion, eh? About our captain's state of mind?"

"No." The dance floor got more crowded. Where was Luke?

"Dear, loyal Kitty. The captain is a lucky man. I'd give the world and all its gold to have you on my side."

Time to come clean, Kitty thought, cut through the things left unsaid between them. "Alec, I'm sorry. For what I said to you at the funeral. I was horrible. Seeing you alive, in that uniform... I'm not excusing myself, you understand."

"Kitty, I wish my plane had caught the fire that brought Philippe down, just as I wish I'd had someone like you waiting for me. Were that the case, I would have had the good sense not to go, of course. But we did go. And it's why I've gotten to you first, as well." He grinned like a schoolboy with a prize. "I'm now ahead of them all, for once."

"Well, you can tell Jack that Luke's safely tucked away. And not ready to go back."

"Kitty, you cut me to the quick. I don't work for Jack."

"Spare me your distinctions."

His merry eyes sobered. "My concern is for you, my love. Perhaps it's time you left Captain Kayenta to me?"

She tried to see around him, to their table, but he swung her deeper into the crowd of dancers. "You're asking the wrong person, Alec."

"I'm asking the girl I know. While trying to keep my country informed. You Americans and the damned English are carving up vital information, just as you've carved up the sea lanes-- with no regard for Canada's sovereignty! Kitty, this spy network has cut down six of my countrymen and two of you Yanks already."

"So, Luke did you a favor, there at the watch shop?"

"He did indeed."

"Return it, Alec. Leave us be."

His face reddened, but his voice remained calm. "Jack is giving you a crash entry into the O.S.S., Kitty. It's wartime, special circumstances, I know all that. Still, I would have never gotten you involved. I would have respected Philippe's wishes."

Kitty watched her shaking hand press Alec's shoulder. "Don't take it out on Jack. It was almost an accident, how I got involved."

"Well. The water's getting deeper." He sighed elaborately as he swung her into the cheek to cheek embrace of the dance. "I'll be standing by. That's a promise, love."

Kitty heard a strange sound, like a muffled explosion. Alec stopped dancing. His arm shot out, placing a sudden, wide distance between them. His eyes went glassy. A woman behind him screamed.

His mouth struggled to form another word as it filled with blood.

Chapter 14

Kitty felt a hard push that knocked her off her feet, then an iron grip at her waist. Panicked, she struggled until she heard Luke Kayenta's voice at her ear. "Come," he commanded, half-carrying her against the current of swarming people.

The blare of police sirens sounded. Blue-coated officers blocked one exit. Another. Luke's hold tightened.

A small, hissing sound was followed by, "Hey. Boy Scout." Kitty tensed as one of their waitress's hands gripped Luke's sleeve, another shoved Kitty's pocketbook at her middle. Linked, the three snaked their way to a corridor behind the bandstand.

Kitty turned. "Wait. We have to get Alec."

"Come," Luke said again, looking between her eyes, not into them. She felt robbed of the steady calm of his direct gaze. Yes, that was how it was at Rumplemeyer's. Was Alec dead?

The waitress led them into a porcelain and steel blur of a kitchen. There, another, slower paced world existed, out of joint with Kitty's rushed breathing. White-aproned men calmly cut sandwiches. A tweed-capped guy drank coffee in a doorway.

"Go through the delivery entrance," their waitress said, nodding behind the short-order cooks. "Abie the breadman might run a couple of passengers downtown, won't you love?" she asked the man in the doorway.

Abie grinned. "Anything for you, Disa," he said, taking a last gulp and handing her the cup. More sirens sounded. "Let's go, folks."

Outside, Luke steadied Kitty as she flung her pocketbook's strap over her shoulder and climbed into the truck.

"Take good care of her, Boy Scout," Disa said.

"Yes, ma'am," Luke responded, as dutifully as one.

As he followed Kitty, the waitress's eyes flashed. Something she did in that instant made a small twitch dance in Luke's cheek. Kitty looked past him, where Disa offered her a small wave, looking like the cat that caught the canary. The delivery man, chuckling, started the truck's engine.

As their ride rumbled down pothole-infested Tenth Avenue, Kitty breathed in wooden crates, bread and waxed paper. She counted the descending numbered streets. The driver shouted back at them amiably. "Whee! Cops swarming all over the joint. Reminded me of Prohibition days. Speakeasys to dim-outs. Never a dull moment, even for the bread man! My last stop's down on Twelfth Street," he informed them. "All-night diner for the meat packers. Not a good area for your girl, son. Shall I drop you off someplace sooner?"

"Thirty-third, please," Kitty said.

Abie threw a package down at them as they stood at the corner of a deserted, warehouse-lined street. Silvercup Bread. The brand her mother bought. Somehow, having something familiar in her hands soothed Kitty's jangled nerves. Luke's silence, his hooded eyes sure weren't helping.

"You are very kind," he thanked their driver.

"Naw. I just owe Disa a few favors," Abie replied. "Curfew's serious after one a.m., even in this crazy town. Get off the streets now," he advised.

Kitty felt Luke Kayenta's breathing as he pulled a pocket watch's chain from his vest, popped open the face, started at the dial, then tucked it away again. They watched the truck rumble on.

"What did she do?" Kitty asked, feeling the warm summer night air, infused with the machine oil scent of the area's daytime activity.

"Do?"

"Disa. When you were getting on the truck. What did she do to embarrass you?"

"Oh. She. Ah..."

"She goosed you, didn't she?"

"Goosed?"

"Pinched your rear end."

"Yes. Why? What does that mean?"

"The hussy." A splintered laugh burst out of Kitty. "She beat me to it." Another laugh. Strange, stuttering, ending in a sob. She tried to stop it with her hand, but it exploded between her shaking fingers. Kitty didn't know if she was laughing or crying or about to throw up on his nice new suit.

Luke looked into her eyes. Finally. Into her eyes, not between them. Why had she needed that so badly? She didn't like what she saw now.

"Kitty."

"Alec was bleeding. Out of his mouth, before I lost hold of him, before I fell. That's not good, is it?"

"No."

She stumbled backward. He took her arms. "Breathe, Kitty."

She felt her forehead touch his vest.

"Breathe," he urged again.

She obeyed, pulling tobacco and her own cologne into her lungs. She felt the soothing, now familiar feel of his breath coursing over her scalp.

"I told him that..."

"Slowly," he whispered.

She inhaled, and began again "I told him I was sorry, for screaming, blaming him at Philippe's funeral. I told him."

"That's good." He stroked her hair.

"I saw his arm, waving me back, before I fell or, did someone knockeme down? Where were you? What was he saying, about you? I can't think."

"It does not matter."

"It does! He was looking out for us! He was always doing that, looking out for Philippe and me. I didn't answer his letters, I didn't return his phone calls. Seven, Mama said. He tried seven times."

"You made peace with him tonight."

"Not enough!" A wail erupted. Then tears. Flowing. At last. All the tears she hadn't shed. For

Alec, for Philippe, for the baby. She couldn't stop them. They streamed over her hands, over the white waxed paper wrapping the bread. The dense blackness of Luke Kayenta's suit absorbed them. They dissolved into the starch of his shirt. They echoed back from the bricks of the warehouse wall.

Her tears were not for this grimy, desolate place. He shouldn't see them, hear them, this stranger who shouldn't matter as much as he did, who would surely follow Alec, Philippe, the baby, leaving her alone again. She had to pull them back, the tears. They were not for him. Why did he stand there as she burrowed, pulling open his vest, clawing past his suspenders to the white shirt with a crazy intensity, to reach his skin?

He allowed it. Allowed it all, even her fingers strafing his hairless chest. His damaged, bandaged middle was just below it. What was she doing?

"Oh God. Luke, I'm so sorry."

"It's all right. Just breathe. Please, Kitty. Just keep breathing."

The desperation in his voice broke through her shame. Breathe? She was a nostrils-flaring madwoman taking great gulps of air, breathing too much. But he didn't mean breathe, not that only. He was talking about living. This strong, brave man was unnerved. He was pleading with her to live. How young he is, Kitty thought. He should be in his mountains, with his sheep, not in the shadows of a Tenth Avenue warehouse, with me.

"That's it" he crooned. "In. Out." His big, shepherd's hands cleared hair back from her forehead. Calm hands. She took one of them between hers, kissed into the palm, began tracing its heart line with her tongue.

The rush of embarrassed color that Disa had inspired flooded his face again. Kitty breathed a soft pattern from his shoulder blade to the large pink scar over his heart. Had they tried to burn out that heart?

She heard an animal sound somewhere between a growl and a snarl. It made her think of the zoo's panthers, were they free. Then Luke took her waist between those large hands and lifted her against the brick warehouse wall. The movement felt like a dance step between them. And he danced so well. Had she told him that before Alec came between them and the latest madness started? Luke slid his knee between her legs, anchoring her. She felt a rush of anticipation. Endless kissing between them, as he pressed closer, pinning her against the brick, growing hard against her thigh.

When she came up for air, his mouth -- hot wet, descended down her neck. The pads of his thumbs made circles under her breasts. She wove her fingers through his hair and watched stars she'd never seen in her city, not before the war and its blacked-out skies. She did not feel diminished below them, not when this man was doing these things.

Her hand found his thigh. He growled out her name in that way only he pronounced it, both languid and hard and, this time, a question. Kitty nodded her answer, pressed against the coursing rhythm of his heart. Yes. She wanted to hike up her skirt there, against that wall and welcome him inside that desolate, empty place she'd only thought of as a wound for so long.

But as she groped for her dress's hem, a white flash blinded her.

Chapter 15

Luke turned, drew his gun. Kitty blinked to clear purple spots. From under Luke's protective arm, she made out a large camera, with a smiling, portly man in a pin-striped suit, the stub of a smoking cigar in his mouth standing behind it. The only concession the man made to the danger he was now in was to lower the camera.

"Ah, New Yorkers!" he proclaimed. "Infusing the war-dark night with joy! Not afraid to laugh, cry or make love right on our streets. Congratulations. You have had the honor of being unmasked for a photograph in my upcoming volume, The Naked City!"

It was a garrulous voice, a face Kitty had known since childhood. "Luke," she urged, tugging his iron arm, "He's all right. Everybody knows him. He used to play the violin at the movie theaters before talkies."

The man placed his thumb and smallest finger to his temples and squinted.

"Let me see...Mrs. Berry's younger daughter. No popcorn, two pickles per show."

"How did you remember, Mr. Fellig?"

"Remember, nothing! And no more Fellig, my dear! I am now called Weegee the Psychic. I know all and see all! Premonitions of crimes and fires, my specialties, though I can conjure from past lives as well. But, but, but... tonight only, I'm willing to pitch in here, for you, and for the war effort."

"Pitch in?"

"Isaiah Morgenstern and I grew up together, lieb. Baram Gershom, may he rest in peace, he was a good friend to my father. Anyone who brings down his killers, gets little Kitty Berry on the dance floor again, not to mention makes both cops and Hoover's boys fall over themselves in pursuit? Well, he is a friend of mine too, maybe." He took a draw on his cigar. "Listen. I got some things to tell you, if you'll be good enough to stand down, Captain."

Kitty turned, looked up at Luke's set mouth. He replaced his gun in its holster. But his eyes never left Arthur Fellig.

"Talk," he commanded gruffly.

Weegee frowned. "You want to take better care of food, with the world at war."

"Food?" Luke slowly took the bread man's battered gift jammed between his shirt and vest. He rolled his eyes before pitching it back into Kitty's keeping.

* * *

The man who'd stolen their image reminded Luke of one of the sacred clowns of his people, from his dancing eyes to his playful, bowlegged walk as he led them to the back of his car. This man knew Isaiah Morgenstern. So, he was not an enemy, but another ally in this city that filled him with wonder and confusion.

Weegee lifted the rounded lid of his car's trunk to reveal a typewriter, police radio, newspaper clippings, photographs and camera equipment. Luke found himself drawn, almost against his will, to the photographs, as the sacred clown spoke around the cigar in his mouth.

"Yeah, I got there pretty soon after. Hoover's boys complained about you not leaving one for them to interrogate. That's gratitude for you, eh?"

In the photographs, the faces of the men Luke had killed were grim, angry. Were their chindi looking to infect him with their ghost sickness? Luke felt a line of sweat form along his back.

"Are the police looking for us, Mr. Fellig?" Kitty asked.

"Well, it's like this, kids. Hoover's boys and a guy who usually sells perfume to society dames did some fancy talking at the crime scene, the downtown, lower-east side one, I mean: at Morgenstern's shop. Their arguments weren't working too well, so they go uptown to continue the discussion. There, at the police station, another hell breaks loose. APB came in over the radio: a domestic murder uptown, with one of their own fleeing the scene."

"One of their own?"

"Yeah, a cop from your neighborhood, Kitty. On the make for years. Nolan."

"Nolan?" Kitty whispered.

"A bad apple. Catting around with a new girlfriend. Maybe she threatened to spill the beans to the wife. Maybe not. He strangled her, but not before she put in a call to the cops. Waitress at the Westminster."

"Oh God. Alice."

Kitty touched Luke's arm, their first contact since the photographer had caught their image. Grateful, Luke covered her hand as the man's eyes sobered.

"You knew her? Gee that's tough, kid. We both lost friends tonight."

Alice. The woman with dancing eyes, serving him food, telling Kitty to take him to Rumplemeyer's, she was not a friend, Luke realized. He and Kitty had always been shadowed by this woman, now dead, at the hands of her lover, the beat cop with hate in his eyes.

Not Jack Spenser, then, after them? Not the O.S.S.? Was he keeping distance from the wrong people? Who were Alice and Nolan connected to? Luke struggled to keep his enemies numbered. He had only enemies and allies in this place. He had no friends, except her, the woman holding his arm, even after what he'd almost done.

He'd meant to comfort, only to comfort her in her fine, howling grief, not to...what did the belegaana call it? Take advantage of her. Kitty Charente should not now be pressing herself closer to his heart. But she was. He offered thanks for it as he held her closer and listened to the sacred clown.

"There's something rotten at the downtown station house, more rotten than the usual rotten, I think," the man began. "Nolan, he's a red-baiter, that's how he got pulled off duty on the Lower East Side, coming down hard on the Slavs, the Jews, thinks we're all Communists and anarchists. After strangling the girlfriend, Nolan gathers up a bunch of off-duty, renegade cops to protect him. Up to Harlem they go. Holy Hannah, I'm following all this, see, on the police radio. Sometimes I think they forgot they gave me permission to have one here in the Chevy. Or maybe they think I sleep at night, like a normal person. Well, Nolan may have gone bad, but he's still one of their own. And his pals, maybe they're just loyal, and dumb as dirt. So it still shocks me, you know, the order from the precinct."

"What order?" Luke asked.

"That Nolan's armed and extremely dangerous. Shoot to kill. So now there's two batches of cops, in a place it's easy to cover up a situation, so it's looking like a civil war up there. People would ask questions about this anywhere else. But not in Harlem, see? So, I smell a rat. Like somebody doesn't want Nolan alive to sing out. Well, that's all I know, kids. Radio's been quiet after that. Too quiet, if you ask me."

Luke planted a kiss on Kitty's forehead. "Let's check on the children," he said.

A smile shifted the cigar in the photographer's mouth. "Should I drive you? Stand by?"

"Why do you trust me?" Luke asked quietly.

"Isaiah Morgenstern told me to, son. Says you're a prize that a number of bad characters want. Can't let that happen. Not in my city."

There was no place safe, Luke thought. But he could do this, get Kitty home, at least.

Once the one who called himself Weegee left them off two streets from where Kitty and her family lived, Luke sighted the O.S.S. watchers in the black car, parked at the side of her building. They were both asleep. Luke felt his anger flare. Why didn't the O.S.S. get better men to watch over her family? Jack Spenser had a deep debt to the airman's wife. There. Good, think of her that way again. The airman's wife. Not Kitty, who mattered, who had his heart. Whose chances would be better without him?

Luke nodded toward the car. "We must get past those two. Walk on the balls of your feet," he instructed.

"I can't," she whispered back. "Heels too high."

"Give me your shoes."

She obeyed in silence. He hooked them behind his suspenders.

They approached the building. He nodded. She opened the door. He slipped in first and scanned the space. Empty, but for the memory of the day before, when she'd first placed her mouth over his. He motioned her in.

"Your family sleeps in different places," he said.

"Three apartments, yes. I have the keys."

"We should check them all, maybe?"

She nodded, climbing the stairs ahead of him.

Her parents' home came first. Luke followed close behind her as she walked toward their open bedroom door, and glanced over the couple spooned together on the bed. The moon's light made Kitty's mother's beautiful braid shine silver, reminding him of his grandmothers'.

They climbed to the third floor. Her brother's wife slept in the first room, like a mother bear protecting her cubs, who were deeper inside the den. Two beds there, but the boys slept in one, Matty nesting in the curve of his brother's back. Luke smiled in relief.

Kitty's shadow left, but he lingered. Then he heard a gasp. He turned. Kitty had walked too close to her brother's wife. The flame-haired woman sat up, her eyes wild.

"You two are in such trouble," she said. Luke stepped back.

"What do you mean, Molly?" Kitty asked.

"Well, I don't mean pranks, or even an argument with Jimmy Walker's nephew this time! Berrys can find jams in their sleep, my mother warned me when I took up with your brother. Well, I wish you'd leave my boys out of this one. It took your Mr. Spenser to release Dom and Matty from the station house, then he and his fancy Kraut doctor grilled them for twice as long here!"

Luke felt the child called Matty approach and stand beside him. Luke opened his palm for the small fingers that took refuge there. "Aunt Kitty. Luke. I didn't crack, honest," Matty said. "Didn't tell nobody nothing. Dom and me, we outlasted them."

Luke looked at the stuffed animal, half the boy's size, dangling from his grip. Bear. The protective spirit again, was guarding this family.

Kitty crouched and then reached out her arms for the boy. He dove into them, something he had done before, Luke thought, this was a ritual between them. Luke alone now bore the brunt of the mother bear's damning gaze.

"Who are you?" Molly Berry demanded. "What have you brought into my family?"

"The war," Luke said quietly.

A sudden thump sounded from the floor above.

"Good God, now what?" the woman intoned.

Luke held up his hand to silence her, as he listened to the pattern of beats coming through the ceiling. "Distress," he said.

"Anya and Zala! Shall I call..."

"No calls," he commanded both women. "Stay."

Chapter 16

Kitty followed him, slipped while climbing the stairs, slamming her hip into the railing and tearing her nylons. This man was hell on stockings.

He'd forgotten about keys again. Didn't anybody lock up where he came from? So, she wasn't ignoring his order. He needed the key. But when Kitty looked down the hall to her sister's corner apartment, the door was open. The silence echoed in her ears until she heard Luke's quiet voice, followed by gruff, staccato responses. And laughter. Cruel laughter.

Two sounds came in quick succession. The first, wasps flying. The next: gunfire.

In the living room, a uniformed policeman looked stunned. He fell to his knees, then to his face on the floor. Oh God, Kitty thought. Where was Luke? She spotted him in the shadows, returning his weapon to its holster with that unholy calm.

Kitty approached. Luke's hand, hot, smelling of gunpowder, reach for her cheek. "Take care of your sister," he said.

"My sister?" Kitty followed his glance and saw Anya, so still, on the floor. She knelt, touched her sister's throat, then heard a calm voice, her own, instruct. "Call for an ambulance."

"We already have."

Kitty turned to see two men in rumpled suits standing in the doorway. Jack Spenser's men, from the black car. Not sleeping now. How did they get upstairs so quickly?

"Mrs. Charente..."

"My sister never asked for any of this!"

"Yes, Ma'am," one of the men said, falling back. He looked to his partner, who was now kneeling beside the fallen policeman. Checking for a pulse, shaking his head. Dead policeman. "Don't touch him any more," the first said. "You know how they get when they think we're interfering with the investigation of one of their own."

The second man stood, pushing his hat back off his forehead. "What happened here, Mrs. Charente?"

"I'm not sure."

She turned to where Luke had been. He was gone.

"I see."

But they hadn't seen. Hadn't seen Luke Kayenta at all, and now he was gone. How was that possible?

She heard banging on the bedroom's door. Kitty approached, opened it. Zala flew into her arms. "Aunt Kitty! You heard my dashes and dots, Morse code, just like they taught us at school."

"Yes." Luke had heard. She had not.

The wail of the ambulance sounded from the street. Kitty couldn't shield her niece from all this, only hold her. "Help's coming. Come, take your mama's hand, sweetie," she urged. When she did, Anya moaned. Her bruised cheek shook with effort until one eye opened.

"Don't go," Anya pleaded.

"We've got you," Kitty whispered. "We've got you now."

Soon St. Vincent's Hospital had her sister ringed by doctors, nurses, family, all surrounded by police guards, with plainclothesmen among them. Some Kitty recognized as Jack's men. How could they tell true guardians from those who would assault a woman? How could she tell?

Kitty wanted her sister to open her eyes again, to tell a story, to crack a joke. The voice of her boss came with a deep shadow of weariness, behind her.

"You need some sleep."

"I'm staying," Kitty told Jack Spenser and his companion, Dr. Saltzman.

Jack's voice tightened. "Listen to me, Kitty. This is bad. The police are furious. One kill shot fired, at an officer."

She frowned. "After he got an innocent woman to open her door, then brutalized her."

"They are saying the officer was coming to her aid, Mrs. Charente," Dr. Saltzman countered.

"Who is saying that?" she demanded.

Jack stepped closer. "That's the official story. The brave officer who never had a chance."

"No one heard more than one shot." Saltzman said quietly. "Did you?"

"No," she admitted, remembering the wasp sounds, trying to turn the cruel growls she'd heard into words.

"Kitty, my man said he smelled gun powder on you."

She laughed. "Well, case closed. I killed that noble cop."

Jack lowered his voice. "Listen to me! Some of my own people are advising that we should let the police hunt Luke down. That he has to be sacrificed."

"I'm sure you agree, Dr. Saltzman," Kitty said.

"Not at all, dear lady."

Kitty's attention returned to her sister. "Anya will tell them what happened. They can't twist their lies around that."

"Your sister's suffered a trauma."

"Anya will remember." But Kitty sounded less sure, even to herself. The silence among them lingered over three of her sister's deep, even breaths. Jack Spenser broke their silence.

"Where is he, Kitty? I still believe in that boy. I won't help them bring him down. But we're spun out, way out of control. You must get him in."

"He's not a boy."

Jack's long fingers pressed her arm. "Do me one favor, would you? Listen to your mother."

Kitty followed his look to the woman standing in the doorway. She walked over, wrapped her arms around her mother's waist.

"Your papa is organizing Mabel, Louis, Harold and Buddy to pitch in here, run errands, get food, spell us for shifts," she said while stroking Kitty's hair back from her temple. "We got cousin Theresa from the East Side watching the children. So. Look, milada. What I brought for you. A washcloth, towel, some nice gardenia soap from home. You need to go, wash your face, rest a little. Our Anya, she won't be alone, Kitty. Not for a minute. So, go."

"Mama..."

"Go with God, Kitty."

Her mother's no-nonsense voice was edged with, what was it, fear? Kitty stumbled into the hospital ladies' room. A crisply uniformed nurse stood before its bank of mirrors, touching up her lipstick. She looked over Kitty's rumpled purple satin dress and ruined stockings through the reflection.

"A wild night?"

Kitty only managed a quick nod, as she opened the spigot. She filled the basin and soaked the washcloth, then pressed the wet cloth against her face and neck.

"Did you lose these?" the woman asked, opening her hand.

Kitty looked down at her own gleaming engagement ring and wedding band. The nurse placed them in her palm.

"We should always have a good eye for diamonds, no matter where they land, yes?" The nurse was familiar, her voice, accented French. Not Philippe's Canadian patois, but from-France French. And her finger nails were long and painted red.

She smiled slowly. "I like the calm, quiet places like this, where the men do not come. Where we may say what we like, while they think we are only making ourselves more beautiful for them."

"Isabelle," Kitty realized.

"Yes. Isabelle Marius. I was at table earlier this evening, at a gathering of old friends. Behind Morgenstern the watchmaker's shop. I was not supposed to rise from that table. But I did rise, to fight another day, because of you, because of our Luke. And now, I would like to help you."

"Help?"

"Yes, cherie. And perhaps you would like some of the cool night air? Without the company of all these doting men?" She laughed. "Sometimes great beauty is a curse, no?"

Kitty smiled, in spite of herself, at a woman who was so full of life in this dark place.

"C'est bon!" Isabelle Marius approved. "Now, first, you must become not so colorful. An exchange. My uniform perhaps?"

"But, I'm not a nurse."

"Oh, neither am I!" she said with a blithe wave of her hand. "Though when the S.S. officers, they marched into my beautiful city, my city of light, I wished to know how to relieve them of some cherished parts of their bodies with my kitchen knife. Perhaps I will take it up some day, this nursing, this surgery even. Come," she urged, as she unhooked ugly white cotton stockings from the most gorgeously black laced garter belt Kitty had ever seen.

"You like? Well, borrow this too. It has little pockets, see? This side for the bribes--" she showed Kitty the edges of two one hundred dollar bills. "This, for the phone call." Kitty saw the outline of a nickel. "And this--" Now the Frenchwoman showed the small sheathed dagger that snugly reinforced the back strap of the garter belt. "This is for the big trouble. You will wear it all, yes, Agent Charante?"

Their exchange was almost complete when Kitty thought of only one other thing she needed. She rifled through her battered pocketbook until she found Matty's baseball card, the one she'd promised to deliver to Luke. Isabelle Marius' bright eyes lit further. "Ah, très bien, the Yankee's horse of iron!" she proclaimed. "Another angel to guide our Ange de Lumière."

"What does that mean?" Kitty asked.

"Why, angel of light. Do you not see our Luke so?"

"Yes," Kitty realized as she said it.

"Good." Another of her dazzling smiles lit Isabelle's face. "Now to the styling of our hair," she said, pulling pins from the nurse's cap and letting down the austere style that did not suit her. "My top knot to trade for this chic soft bob of yours."

Kitty felt panic rising into her throat as she placed the baseball card against her thigh and latched the garter belt over it.

"Ah, now," Isabelle breathed with her. "Sit here, before the mirror. While I work." The elegantly polished fingers began weaving through Kitty's hair as the melodious voice continued. "Life is short and very dangerous in times of war, no? Luke perhaps needs the supplies I have packed in your nurse's medical bag. Your dear mama tells me your hands are most healing. And Philippe would want his clever Kitty to be happy, would he not? Please. Let me take your place, cherie. Allow me to sit vigil with your mama, while you find our dear shepherd, yes?"

Kitty's mother waited as they walked from the washroom. The senior Katherine Berry nodded, then took Isabelle's arm and led her back to Anya's room. The men's eyes followed them, allowing Kitty to dissolve into the working machine of the hospital. She was not sure of herself, even less as she checked her cap and drew the regulation navy blue cape about her shoulders outside. The uniform gave her a pass through the dimmed-out city, she realized as her breathing tightened. Walk. Isabelle had said to walk, so she did.

The shoes Kitty had exchanged with the Frenchwoman's hurt her feet-- too small, especially with the thick stockings. The '38 Chevy cruised slowly, matching her steps.

"Say, I'm a good taxi service, in a pinch, Kitty Berry," the driver called over.

She breathed easy. "Well, that's what I'm in, Mr. Fellig."

"A pinch? How so?"

"I don't know where I'm going."

"Need to think?"

"Exactly."

"I drive, you think."

"Deal."

Her father smoked two cigars every Sunday afternoon, so the scent of Weegee's stub made Kitty feel safe, protected. The silence between them lasted until they were in the Garment District, where the car was the sole moving vehicle on the deserted streets.

"Ah, good," her driver proclaimed, "no followers."

Kitty sat up straight, looked out the back windshield. "I didn't even wonder."

"Hmmm. Neither did he. What kind of outlaws are you?"

"He?"

"My previous passenger, the one who kisses you like you're his last meal. I'm worried about him."

"Me too," she admitted.

"So. You got something for him, under that cape?"

She felt the heat rise to her cheeks. "Mr. Fellig!"

He rolled his eyes. "I mean something for his hurt, you know, a nurse something."

"Hurt? Luke's hurt?"

"I'd say so. Got nothing out of him about it, though. Just grunts, a little blood on the seat, and thanks, when I let him off. He's polite, anyway. But we didn't have a good start. Earlier, I mean. I don't think he likes his picture being taken."

"Where did you let him off?"

"I thought you'd never ask. It was the first question out of that swanky French dame, who promised she could get you out of St. Vincent's with no one the wiser. Fellow nurse, I take it?"

"Mr. Fellig!"

"All right, all right, you agents never have time for a proper chat! Columbus Circle, at the park, I let him off. Any idea where he'd go from here?"

Kitty leaned over, kissed his stubbled cheek. "I do. Thanks, Mr. Fellig. Thanks a million."

Chapter 17

Luke Kayenta left his shoes under the park's lamp, at a crossroad in Central Park, a spot he and Kitty had passed on their way to the zoo. He began his climb on the rock formations, a good place to die. Bats sifted by him as he climbed, feasting on the warm night's insects, sensing so much better than he did into the dark reaches. A raven called him like a brother. Raven, the prophet bird, was also dressed in black. There would be death, so much more death in this war. Like all wars, it would spin out of control of belegaana men who thought they could control everything.

But these things were not his concern. Not any more. He had done his best.

He reached a ledge that was cool and dry. Luke pulled out his pouch and sprinkled a circle of corn pollen. Wetness at his side, his life's blood. Never mind it. Concentrate on the ceremony. He opened one of the already-rolled cigarettes, removed its tobacco, placed it carefully in the middle of his corn circle. Finally, he placed the eagle's feather, anchored by a blue stone.

What else? Something of Kitty, her family. The card. He searched his pockets. Where was Matty's baseball card? Think. Had he left it in the other suit? Well, summon the generosity of the child who'd made him feel like a human being again. And of the child's aunt, who'd made him feel like a man worthy of a woman's love.

This place called for a chant, but no songs came to his dry throat. Luke saw Kitty standing by her sink again, offering him water. Who was the man at her sister's apartment, the one he'd killed? Too confusing, too many enemies. He saw Kitty's sister on the floor. Too late. He'd been too late, again, as he was for his clan brother in Spain and the gentle candle maker, and the Canadian agent.

Luke lay on his back on the rock, facing the stars. Big Bear chased Little Bear across the sky, even here in New York City, where everything else was so strange. The stars were like this in the fourth night of his fasting when he was a boy seeking manhood. His head now felt soft, porous as it had then, when his vision came, along with his animal guide. His mother, his grandmother, all his relations saw the same stars tonight. When he died here, would his women say he'd run a good race, like they said about his grandfather? The air felt hot, even with the night breezes. Or was it fever? Whatever it was, it helped him feel the sheep, the past sheep, who had loved this place. They were all around him. Another season descended over this one. Winter, cooling him with lightly falling snow.

And sheep. Belled, docile, too fat, overfed by delighted children, Kitty among them. She was not yet the airman's wife, not yet a woman. There, the one who had touched him with her courage, her love medicine, was a child, smaller than Matty. Giggling, dressed in a coat the tinted rose color of his painted desert home. The coat, the black curls began moving away from him now, swallowed by the fleecy coats of the belled sheep. Come back. Please, Kitty. Don't leave me here, so out of balance. She turned, looked up, at him. Those eyes, even so young, recognized a stray. She took his hand, welcomed him over the ridge.

There, another vision began. Luke entered into that one, with her, his heart singing.

* * *

Kitty saw his shoes hanging from the lamppost. She shook her head, then stuffed them into her wide-mouthed nurse's bag. Yes, she knew those lost Valentino eyes of his would seek out the familiar here. She'd shown him the Sheep Meadow from the eighty-sixth floor of the Empire State Building. When? Yesterday. And a lifetime ago. Well, it might be a good place to hide, Shepherd, she thought, but not from me.

Kitty kicked off her borrowed, too-tight shoes, but left on the horrible white stockings, still attached to Isabelle Marius' mantrap garter belt. Had Luke ever seen that lacy concoction she now wore? She stretched out her cramped toes, thinking of his helpless look when she'd caught him eyeing her legs. And realized she loved the way it had made her blood race.

Well, that man wasn't happy unless he was climbing, so she swung her bag over her shoulder and looked for a pass in the rocks. He might be a good climber, but he was in her territory. She had scrambled over these ridges many times with her brothers. An unearthly shriek shook her balance. Easy. Animals were close by, in Central Park Zoo, she reminded herself. A black feather, reminding her of the coats of the panthers, and Luke Kayenta's hair, suddenly floated down. He'd laugh, when she told him about her panic, about forgetting about the zoo's animals close by.

Their cages must be awful for them, especially in the dark. It had been better for the sheep, used to human company and with their meadow to roam. She remembered as a child, feeling like Mary Had a Little Lamb among them. Then the Depression hit, and the park became a dangerous place after dark, for fat sheep. For women, too. That was years ago, she chided herself, not now, keep climbing. A little higher. Luke was here, she knew it. He was not dangerous, not to her. And not crazy. She would find him. He would tell her why he shot that policeman.

When she saw him lying so still, Kitty's pounding heart stopped. She moved closer. Deep, even breathing. She was prowling Central Park, with the roars and yelps of zoo animals for company, while he slept? She saw the yellow dust of his corn pollen on the pads of his fingers. She snorted softly, but hiked her skirt and retrieved the baseball card she'd promised Matty to return to him from Isabelle's garter belt. She placed it into his hand, and closed his fingers over it.

"Hey, Shepherd," she tried calling him awake. His eyelids flickered. She knelt, lifted his head onto her lap. She opened her pack, found the flask, held it to his lips. "Drink," she demanded.

"I am fasting, no drink," he murmured. His eyes finally opened. His nostrils flared. "And no women." He was staring past an opened button of her uniform, at the lace of her slip, the sheen of sweat between her breasts. He closed his eyes, groaned. Kitty spied the bulge in his pants.

"Jeepers, men! It's the damn first and last to everything isn't it?"

Luke blinked once, twice. His voice was a scrape against metal. "You should not be here. Distracting me," he groused, "I'm busy. Go away."

"Busy? Busy doing what?"

"Dying."

She grabbed a hold of a hank of his hair. "Oh no you don't, Luke Kayenta. Not on my watch. Drink!" She forced the watered whiskey down his throat. He coughed, but didn't spit it out. Then he stared hard at her. "Kitty?"

She frowned. "Who else would be foolish enough to..."

"Not your scent, Kitty."

He'd smelled Isabelle Marius. That French woman's scent had made him hard?

"I ask your pardon," he whispered now, his voice pained. Kitty realized that she still had a hold of his hair. She opened her fingers. "Nothing to be sorry for, you were just being a man."

Luke sat up, wincing, then noticed the baseball card in his hand. "The Iron Horse," he said, recognizing the ball player.

"Don't lose it again. You'll hurt Matty's feelings."

He placed the card under a rock that also held the black and white feather that the Empire State window washer had given him. Praying. He'd been praying. Tears welled in Kitty's eyes, unbidden. Luke held her face between those big hands and stared into her soul. "Your sister, she will recover, Kitty. I saw her, living in a fine house by the ocean, with her husband, returned from the war. She was happy. Zala was there, in a blue-flowered dress. And more children."

"What are you saying?"

"It was a place of very fine sand, grasses growing out of it, what are they called? Those sea grasses?"

"Luke, how...?"

"You showed me, led me there, when you were a little girl."

"I... showed you?"

"Yes, from right here." He patted the rock face. You were here, remember? In winter. In the snow. Your coat the color of the dawn sky of a fine day. Losing hold of your mother, going with the sheep, all the way up here. Laughing, fearless. Remember?"

She touched his face. He frowned. "You don't remember?"

"Luke, was this a dream?"

"Yes, a dream, a powerful dream. I saw you. And you led me to your sister, after the war's end, well and happy."

"To Montauk Point, where they bought land and plan to... but, that's not possible. Is it?"

Of course it is, Kitty heard her mother's no-nonsense voice in her head. You think only old

Romani people have the Sight? Take comfort from this boy, who only dreams of you, even when he believes he's at death's door.

Kitty smelled blood. "Luke." She pulled off the blue nurse's cape, set the bag on it. "Let me see where you're hurt." He was staring, confused, at her uniform.

"My ticket out of the hospital," she explained. "Borrowed from your friend, Isabelle Marius."

"Ah."

Kitty set out three bottles. "She's very beautiful."

"And I told you, she has a handsome husband, who loves her, whom she loves."

Kitty cut a length of bandaging. "I hear that doesn't stop French women."

He laughed. She didn't realize how badly she wanted to hear that sound. She offered the flask again. "Mostly water," she lied. "Please, Luke, drink."

He obliged her. Their fingers touched, held, as he returned the flask. She lifted the coat from his shoulders, peeled layers of his clothing back, until one of them stuck to him. She poured the mix of carbolic acid and glycerin onto a cotton ball, then around the wound until the layers of cloth lifted away.

"Kitty," he summoned, both his eyes and voice lazy now under the growing influence of the whiskey. "When you were a little girl in the snow, with the sheep? Your winter coat. The sleeves were folded back."

She avoided his eyes, concentrating on her work. "The coat was a hand-me-down from Anya," she surrendered. "It had been red. It faded to your dawn color."

"Oh, I see."

"You see entirely too much," she said softly, blinking back tears.

"Kitty..."

"I love the beach at Montauk. I hope Anya lets me visit."

His finger grazed her cheek. "You know you'll be welcome."

She bit her lip, and went back to her task of surveying for signs of injury. "That climb didn't do your cuts any good. Opened up three, no, four," she chastised him.

"That's all?"

"More, you want?"

"I'm not shot? Not dying?"

"Shot? This mark on your suit jacket, you mean?" Kitty looked closer. "It's a burn."

He knelt higher, finally looking at his middle. He'd been afraid, she realized. He'd been afraid to look at it. His voice sounded very young. "The bullet is not in me, then?"

"What bullet?"

"At your sister's place."

"I only heard one gun."

"That was my returned fire. The first shots were from a gun with a silencer. An assassin's weapon."

Kitty remembered wasp sounds. "That's not what they said. Cold-blooded murder of a police officer, they said."

"Who said this?"

"Lift your arms."

"Who said it, Kitty?" he pressed, even as he obeyed her.

"Jack," she admitted. "It's what the police told Jack."

"Or what Jack Spenser told the police. So the police might hunt me down, seek their revenge. And he might wash his hands of me."

"No, Luke, listen. Jack's worried. And he believes in you. Even Dr. Saltzman believes in you."

"Quite deeply, Captain."

Luke shoved Kitty behind him.

Too late. One, two, three weapons aimed at his heart, while he'd barely reached his holster.

Chapter 18

What could he offer her now? Only that they would have to go through him first, Luke realized.

"Dr. Saltzman," Kitty called out from behind him. "What are you doing? Where's Jack?"

"Jack has quite found me out, I'm afraid, Mrs. Charente. Due to a Columbia colleague stationed at your unfortunate sister's hospital room. He did not see me as the good Doctor Saltzman, because I am not he. I doubt the doctor's body will ever be found."

He returned his full attention to Luke. "Now, you know your chances are not good, Captain. Let us talk, shall we?"

The speaker wore a crisp new suit, like Luke's. Although his face was now bearded, Luke knew him, from Spain. This was the tall German he and Isaiah Morgenstern had slipped past, as their prison escape descended into chaos. A warrior. One seasoned, calm. And interested. He would use it, this interest, like a weapon, Luke thought, even as the three sharp-eyed marksmen watched him.

Their leader spoke again. "You have sentimental feelings for Mrs. Charente, I gather, Captain?" Precise English. Learned well.

Something else they had in common. "Surrender to us now and she will not be harmed. You do have my word." Behind him, Luke felt Kitty's touch on his sleeve. From the nearby zoo, a panther's cry pierced the night air. The gunmen's stances wavered. They were not as calm as their leader.

"With me," Luke stipulated, "she must stay with me."

"Very well. Now. Might we see your hands, please?"

Slowly, Luke released his hold on the warm leather of his holster and showed his hands. The commander nodded to his men. They moved in, pinned Luke to the rock face. They took his weapon, kept searching, ripped back his bandaging. Kitty screamed her outrage. It blended into the night air with another caged animal's cry. Luke reached for her, but the men shoved him back. He heard his skull crack on the hard blue stone.

The leader advanced. "Achtung! We are not barbarians!" He turned to his captives. "Apologies. My men, they are nervous, Captain, as your reputation did precede you." Cold, precise fingers felt down his leg to his grandfather's knife. The German commander retrieved, then studied it with a thin smile. More interest.

"What fine craftsmanship. The silver, the turquoise inlay. We will speak more of it." His men moved in, blotting out Luke's sight of Kitty, struggling against the two men holding her.

"Rest," their leader insisted now.

Luke felt the sharp stab. Then came the invasion, pumping into his veins, rendering him useless and erasing even the stars.

* * *

Kitty listened to the noises outside the back of the old Ford sedan delivery truck. Two of the bastards who drugged Luke got orders from the bastard who was not Dr. Saltzman. Then they walked off at a fast clip. That left three in the front seat. Cobblestones, broken up streets.

That would be most of the city, since the Depression. Kitty wasn't good at figuring out roads, the subways took her where she wanted to go. But, she thought, maybe the driver wasn't so sure either. Although they exited Central Park speeding, they were cruising more slowly now. Her eyes adjusted to the dim light, bleeding in from cracks and a rust hole over the right rear wheel. Luke stirred, murmured. Kitty leaned over, felt the blood beating at his wrist. At first he'd been so still she feared the worst. Maybe he'd come all the way out of it now, Kitty thought. He mustn't see her like this, crying, disheveled from sacrificing three hairpins to picking the lock of the truck's back door. She leaned over him, and began gently parting his hair with her fingertips.

"Hey, soldier," she whispered.

His glassy eyes struggled to focus. She kept talking. "They took your cigarettes. And everything else— holster, wallet, suspenders, even your shoelaces. What did they think you could do to them with your shoelaces?"

"Kitty. They did not harm you?"

"No. And I've been with you the whole time, too, just like you bargained for."

"How much time has gone?"

"A half hour, maybe."

"We're moving."

"Yes. Two big guys stashed us in an old blacked-out truck. The other two split off. Luke. I heard their leader's name. It's Adler. Do you know him?"

"Yes. Our ways crossed in Spain."

"Old scores to settle now?"

"Well, he could not have been made happy by the work we did there."

Kitty raised her head higher. "I smell fish. If it's from the Fulton Market... yes... those are the planks of the Brooklyn Bridge. We're going over the East River. Want to sit up?"

"Yes."

Kitty felt giddy with a ridiculous joy at the sight of those big shepherd's hands closing around her sleeve. Strange, bursting gulps came out of her, even through her fingers when she tried to stifle them. Luke folded her into his arms, and what was left of her carefully planned brave face dissolved.

"I'm sorry. Kitty, I'm so sorry."

"I'm not. Luke, no matter what happens from here on in, don't worry about that, all right?"

He smiled slowly. "Adits'ah, Yanaha."

"Adit—?"

"Adits'ah. We are in agreement. It is a word in my language."

"That's what they want, isn't it? Words in your language. Adler tried to get you to talk, as you were going under from that needle. He told you to speak, and to translate.

"Did he?" Luke asked quietly.

"You were already too far under. But Adler said you would give him what he wants. He said he had to experiment with the dosage, but you would."

Pain, there, between his eyes. Her words had put it there. But he smiled. "Kitty, I am trained. They cannot get to anything I don't want to give them, do you understand this?"

"I'm not sure."

"I am a soldier, as your husband was, as you are now. These people holding us, they want something that was put into my care."

"The same thing they wanted in Spain?"

"Yes. It is inside me, there is no key. Can you trust me no matter how things seem, when I tell you this?"

"Yes. You can sure dance around a subject, but I don't think you can lie."

"Oh, I can lie."

"And how will I know?"

"This is a good question. We must plan for it. Do you know the story, the one of the tree boy?"

"Tree boy?"

"The story that Mr. Disney made, full of color and movement and song, the one with the father that the whale swallowed?"

"Pinocchio?"

"Yes! That story! When I lie to them, like Pinocchio, my nose will grow."

"But...won't your enemies see it too?"

He laughed. "No. Only you."

The truck hit a series of bumps.

Luke sniffed the air. "Salt."

"Yes, we're near the water."

The sounds came first as eerie whispers, then grew in strength. "A calliope. Barkers." Luke," she summoned him. "Coney Island. We're heading towards Coney Island."

"You know this island?"

"My brothers were lifeguards on the beach there, before the war."

"Of course. The airman, your husband he showed me photographs of you in this place. You know it well?"

"Like the back of my hand."

"This is good."

Chapter 19

Luke heard laughter, turning gears, strange, blasting music, screams. People came here to this place to scream, Kitty told him, speaking too fast. She shifted in his arms now, breathing against his chin, quickening his pulse. Was it possible to fit together so well with a woman? It wasn't only their enjoyment of each other. He took a measureless pride in his fierce, protective lover. He would tell some things to Jack Spenser, if he ever got back in service. He would call Spenser and Spenser's superiors up to Donovan himself what they were: foolish men. This woman they had answering their telephones, displaying her beautiful legs to salesmen and agents; he would tell them she had a warrior's heart. And she had as deep a love for her home and its freedoms as any of them did. Why did they think Kitty Charente couldn't be trusted with their secrets? He inhaled the exotic flower's scent from her hair. If the Germans knew that this woman they too dismissed was the source of his strength, they would separate them, no matter their agreement. What would he do then? Did he really believe his own words to her, that he'd keep the code locked inside him?

Well, he had before, Luke reasoned. Could they do anything worse to him with this drug that had only succeeded in making his world black? Could it be worse than what his Spanish guards had done? The Dinè had no curses, only blessings. So he learned good curses against the Spanish in Isaiah Morgenstern's language. He thought of that time. Who would tell his clan brother's bravery if he didn't return home? No storytellers would keep them alive in the people's memory. Because they were forbidden, even to say the name of the ones who died. Without story, they would both turn to dust faster than anything the Germans could do to him.

Listen, Luke told himself. Listen for the footsteps, approaching the truck. Listen well, the way you did in Spain. You got out of there, you can here. Look for your chance.

Another sound came from the further distance, waves crashing in on the shore. Freedom. Luke's thumb made circles around the weave of Kitty's dress at the shoulders. Circles, sending out warmth, comfort to her skin, to the heart beneath. A heart they shared.

"Kitty," he called softly at her ear. "They are coming. We must try to get away from them."

She nodded. "Shall I toss the medical bag when they open up the back?"

"Yes, good," he agreed to her plan, and watched the door.

It opened. Two. Only two, talking to each other instead of watching them. Did they think their drug was so powerful? Kitty threw the bag, hitting the one on the left. Luke followed, launching himself, head first. He heard a crunch, then a howl. Keep fighting. Get them through. Salt-scented air, from beyond the doorway. But there were too many men in his way. Then, the stars before his eyes. The colorful world beyond the truck's open door slid into a corner and disappeared into blackness.

Chapter 20

Luke was held down by leather straps. He could not even turn his head. People with deep eye sockets but no eyes, dressed in long black coats looked down on him. Luke wondered if he was dead. Through blunted senses, he caught the metallic smell of blood. He fought the panic that rode up his spine.

"Calm yourself, Captain."

The command came from Adler. "Half of what you see are merely vestiges of Dr. Palmer's Law and Order Wax Show. They are here in storage, gathering dust. Now, an attraction called 'The Brooklyn Murder Syndicate' takes center stage. The Americans' popular entertainment degenerates with each passing year. A shame. I remember these figures around us in their better days. It was an amusement set up by Kit Carson's nephew, did you know that? Of course not. You were a child back then, living a life far more exciting than a waxworks show."

"Where is Kitty?" Luke asked, his voice sounding like he was pushing it past wads of wool.

"Why, she is here beside you, as we agreed. Ah, I see the problem. My associates have restrained you more than I would have. But then, your ramming head has not yet cost me a tooth."

Luke heard a muffled growl to his right. Adler pulled open his eyelids again, then shone a pinpoint light. The German's sympathetic "tsk" followed. "I'm afraid my injured men were heavy-handed with your latest dose."

Luke heard Kitty's voice catch, then a sob.

"What are you doing to her?" Luke demanded.

"She has not been harmed. Only made quiet."

Made quiet. What did that mean?

"My fingers are cold," Luke tried.

"That is because you resist the bonds. You could lose all circulation. It would be a shame for such a marksman as you, to return home that way, after this is all over."

Keep him talking, this man who was interested in him. "I herded sheep and goats. I am of no use to you."

"On the contrary. You will be of considerable use. And your business was not sheep, but words, in those distant mountains of Spain. Those words are my business now. Come now, Captain. You wish to return to your desert homeland, do you not? To aim your rifle at the predators of your flock, not at my countrymen?"

"Yes," Luke agreed. The truth. So completely the truth.

"There, now," his enemy consoled him. "You shall go home. We shall be friends again, after the war. And we will protect you, until then. You will return a hero of three nations. Imagine."

Wrong, the images this man was putting into his head. He thinks you are simple. He thinks you desire their foolish medals. Play. Play with that. Luke faced his tormentor. "My superiors, they think I have betrayed them, because I ran, you see?"

"And why did you run, Captain?"

"They thought my mind was ruined. After Spain."

"The clumsy Spanish. They work in brutal, filthy ways, rooted in the past. I saw that room where they held you, Captain. And I saw you during your escape, did I not? On the prison road, in disguise, acting as chauffeur. I knew you for a warrior then. I thought the diplomat was merely coveting the best man for his own protection. It was a clever deception, well executed. We are the future, your people and mine, Captain. You bring invention, we bring discipline. Together we will usher in a new age, a golden age. The Spanish seared your body, did they not? And at my hands, what do you feel now? Any pain at all?"

"No," Luke realized. He felt nothing. He felt disconnected from his body, except for his cold fingertips.

Adler leaned in closer. "That which is running through your veins is helping you to think more clearly, is it not?"

Luke's felt invaded by what this man had forced into his body. Go away from there, he smells your fear. Luke closed his eyes, trying to hear Kitty's breathing, or catch her scent, through the drug, the fear. He heard an order in German, then very cold water on his face. Shocking, choking him. Triggering his rage.

"Dersh tikt zol stu ver'n!" leapt out of him.

"Write it down!" Adler commanded. "Never mind your weapons, he is securely bound. Write! And bring Mrs. Charente closer. Unbind her hands, and his head. Now." Then Adler's voice turned soft, solicitous. "Captain, here is your woman. Can you see her?"

He did. Eyes red, tears running over the ugly black slash of tape covering Kitty's mouth. Luke reached for her, but felt the leather manacles binding.

"Remove the restraint on Mrs. Charente's speech," Adler commanded the guard. He tore at the tape so hard that Kitty's lip bled. But she smiled. How could she smile? How long before the Germans, or the effects of the drug, took her away again? Don't, Luke told himself. Don't think ahead. Stay here, where she was alive, close, restoring his purpose.

"Kitty," he told her. "I am hearing a guide inside my head. Telling me to think towards other possibilities."

"No, Luke. That's the mickey they slipped you, doing the thinking. You don't even sound like yourself. Remember who you are."

Adler took hold of her hair, yanked her head back. Luke heard the swift catch of her breath. "Now, Mrs. Charente. This is not a good way to repay your unmuzzling. You will kindly not speak, yes?"

Luke grabbed for Kitty's hand. Caught it. He held even as Adler leaned over him, frowning. "You Americans discovered this new drug. We were sharing so much about its use before the war. I was working with Dr. Saltzman, in fact, in the wonderful exchanges we had between the wars...learning from each other in precision tools, medicine, eugenics, aboriginal peoples. We, how do you say it? Hit it off quite well. So while Captain Kayenta was recovering in Scotland, I managed to revisit your country. In a more stealthy way this time, of course, because of our unfortunate hostilities. But when I called my old colleague Saltzman, why, he thought I'd never left. No need to come to Chicago, said he, because he was coming to New York, on a very interesting request. To examine the mental state of a young American Indian agent of the government...very hush hush, he could not say more. Well, of course he could spare time for lunch with an old colleague. Oh, dinner? Yes, dinner was an excellent suggestion. Excellent for me as well. So much more can be done in the dark, you see? That's why the good doctor's undoing was much simpler than my quest to find you, Captain. Are you still with us?"

"Yes."

"Good. Now, where were we? These words. The ones you have, and we need. We have a start now, yes?" He took the long brown notebook from the hands of the man whose cheek was swollen. "Let me check if Greer's listening ability is better than his reflexes. "Say them again, please?"

Luke stared at the open page put before his eyes. "All wrong," he said.

"What do you mean?"

"What your man wrote." Luke tried to find the English word. "Gibberish."

"Your language is without an alphabet. Greer recreates it phonetically."

"Not well. This woman can take it down better. She knows the sounds, the cadences, from listening to me."

Kitty's hand went colder there, in his. He turned his head toward her. "My nose. Kitty, it itches. Will you scratch it for me?"

There. Kitty's red painted nails were before his eyes. Red. Like his mother's prayer shawl. "Go longer, will you?" he asked, trying to remind her. "Longer. There. Now write the words, Kitty. They are only words."

"Only words," she repeated. Did she understand?

Adler did not reprimand her for speaking this time, so Luke tried to get a little more out of her. "Yes, words, to end the war faster, to save lives. Still the same purpose they always had."

"But, Luke..." Kitty began.

"There, you do understand, Captain." Adler interrupted her.

"Write, Kitty," Luke urged her darting eyes steady. "You are the one who hears me best. Please."

She took the offered pad and pencil.

"Now," Adler said, impatience creeping into his voice, "this phrase written so imprecisely, that Mrs. Charente will kindly correct. Again, please?"

Luke took in a breath. The leather holding his right hand gave way a little. From the bolt it was attached to, he was sure. An iron bolt. But it had been here, close to shore, in the salt sea air, for a long time. Hadn't Alder said as much? That the wax men display was an old one, in storage from another time?

"Dersh tikt zol stu ver'n," he separated the syllables carefully.

"And what is the meaning, please?" Adler urged, the professor of language now

"It is ... a call."

"A call?"

"Of distress. Mayday. S. O. S."

"I see. Splendid. International. We should all know how to call for help, should we not, Mrs. Charente?"

"Chap a gang," Luke answered for her. "Write it, Kitty. So we can help end the war."

"Chap a gang," Adler repeated, the excitement mounting in his voice. "And what do these words signify?"

"Movement. Fast movement."

"As...of troops?"

"Yes," Luke agreed, to be polite. Not really a lie. That's it, the voice inside him encouraged. Play. Play with the expectations of this belegaana and his magic truth-telling drug. Just as we used to play with the priests, the ministers, the tourists off the Santa Fe railroad. Come to sell us their god, or buy our pots and blankets, remember? Smile. Remember to smile, my brother.

"It's as simple as that, the phrases, nothing hidden within?" Adler asked.

"Well," Luke drawled out slowly. "We are a simple people."

"With an obscure language. Obscure, even to us, who made it our business to study many of you aboriginal people of America. Saltzman and I, we often could find no speakers who were fluent in both."

We were in the boarding schools, Luke realized, the ones who learned to be fluent in both languages. We were children, then. But we are many now. And we are warriors.

"Of course, you are inventive Americans. You would expand, or not use the same languages as you used in the last war." A hard edge crept into his tormentor's voice at the mention of the last war. "The Choctaw, the Cheyenne. I learned the wrong languages. But there are so many." Something terrible had happened to him back then, Luke surmised.

"I'm tired, sir," he tried to draw Adler away from his memory.

"And you'll rest. Comfortably, I promise you, Captain. But Mrs. Charente must fill the paper with phrases first. To convince us that you are worth the danger of a capture. A goal for the two of you. A page of phrases, translations. It is not so hard, is it?"

"No, sir."

"There! Exactly! Are you familiar with the immortal stories of Karl May, Captain?"

"No, sir."

"Well, it may be my great pleasure to acquaint you with them. They are tales of adventure which take place in your own homeland, the great American West. Herr May's books are our leader's favorites, he gave me a copy of one before I embarked on my American adventure all those years ago. Now, when you prove yourself worthy, a reward will be yours, too. A journey across the Atlantic. To us! Where you will be re-educated. A new world will open up to you, then, containing many opportunities. You may become a young Winnetou to my Old Shatterhand in our leader's eyes, if all goes well."

Chapter 21

"Luke," Kitty called softly. "Open your eyes. Please. Talk to me."

From the adjoining room, their radioman moved the dial, spoke into a transmitter. Luke's words, her transcription. God, what had she done?

Stay calm, she told herself. He'd only given them a taste, a page filled, ending with mek haye bobe, which he translated as "end of transmission."

The Germans still needed Luke, there was much more in his head, and they knew it. And once they could get Luke before some recording machinery she'd be useless, except maybe to threaten him, to keep him from changing his mind.

Kitty looked at the stenographer's pad in her hands. She thought of that top sheet covered with words, ellipses, more words. The marks' imprints still bore into the pad like a drill had made them, not a pencil. Mrs. Fry, her first grade teacher, would have slapped her fingers with a ruler for pressing so hard.

Did she have to write the strange words he'd sounded out for her in that drugged, slowed-down

Western whip of a voice? Yes. She had to trust him. She had to believe that she had not betrayed her country. But did Luke expect her to destroy the paper before Adler could transmit it?

Kitty threw the pad in a corner. Luke's eyes wandered, there behind his lids. His right hand again yanked its leather restraint, pulling it taut, slamming the bolt it was attached to against the wood. Kitty heard a crack, a splinter. Adler said something loudly at the same time, so their two remaining guards' attention did not stray from the room beyond. The bolt came through.

Kitty stifled a triumphant laugh at his achievement. But what good would that do if his other arm was secured tight? She took Luke's left hand into hers, squeezed it. His eyes opened, searched the ceiling, then the wax figures around them.

"I'm here," Kitty called softly, moving closer, their noses almost touching. The guards' attention remained with their comrades. She stroked Luke's cheek.

"Ayor anosh'ni, Yanaha," he whispered.

"You don't have to say any more. The page is full." She didn't mean for it to come out as bitterly as it did.

"It is not for the page. It is for you, Kitty."

"What is?"

"What I said. That I love you, Yanaha."

He said it shyly, courageously. She blinked back tears. "Yanaha?"

"The voice, my inside visitor, he has named you this. Yanaha. She Meets the Enemy."

She frowned, glancing toward the adjoining room. "I met him all right. He was at Jack's right hand."

"Jack Spenser did not know Adler's true nature. How could you?"

"That guy in your head is wrong. I caved in, Luke. You had to tell Adler what he wanted, because that's what the drug was doing to you. But I wrote it all down, with the English beside each phase. They have their start on deciphering your code."

"They are in Pinocchio's code, not mine, Kitty."

"Pin—?"

"Didn't I ask you to scratch my nose?"

"Yes, but—"

"Because it was getting longer."

"You were lying? What we gave them, what they're so damned excited about, it was more gibberish?"

"Now, I did not say that. We should get out of here, yes?"

"Out?"

"You know the way? Coney Island is part of your city, yes?"

"Luke, you're locked down to this table."

"And when they want to move us, they will have to unlock me."

"And you pulled the bolt through," she realized. "You have a weapon." She carefully returned the bolt inside the wooden hole.

Luke smiled. "Yes. Watch for it. Watch me, Kitty."

"All right," she said, feeling a smile hurt her lip. "They're coming. Back to sleep, so they keep their damned drug at bay. Good night," she whispered, giving his chin a nuzzle. A beard had started there, finally, after the three days, the lifetime, they'd spent together.

Adler approached. He drew the stethoscope from his pocket and listened to Luke's chest. "As I thought. Quite depressed yet. Another injection at this time might have unfortunate results."

Then Adler said something in German, pointing at Luke. His men hesitated. He threw up his hands, exhaling. "Mrs. Charente. My men are reluctant to approach your captain, who, although he has decimated our numbers, is not so lethal in his present state. An amazing drug, this barbiturate," Adler continued. "Look at him. He knows nothing, can feel nothing. Watch. I'll demonstrate to you, and ease the consternation of my nervous compatriots."

Kitty watched as Adler brought forth Luke's own beautiful knife and placed it against his cheek.

"Don't!" she called out.

"So pale, Mrs. Charente. No need. Under the influence, he will only feel this later. My men were not so fortunate under his attack." He cut a thin line from Luke's cheekbone to his jaw. "There. Not even a twitch. And now his noble bronze face bears the imprint of a seasoned warrior. I am honored to bestow the mark."

Luke's eyes remained closed. But one was tearing, mixing with the blood of his wound. Distract them from it. "Who is the barbarian now?" she shouted. Adler caught her arm in mid-swing. She glared at him, without backing down. "Butcher," she accused.

"An upstanding, useful profession, especially in a world so full of deficiency. Now you, Madame Charente, have instructed me well. American mongrel amateurs are worse than irritating. Their actions are so unpredictable as to threaten the most well-thought plans. I will remember this. Fortunately, unlike our captain," Adler said as he handed her off to the guard on his right, "you are becoming increasingly non-essential. Hold her," he commanded the man, while the remaining two flanked him.

Adler made a concise wave to his men. "Oh, do stand aside. I am in no danger from our brave Red Indian or his woman. Once I release his restraints, we will take our prize home."

He began at Luke's feet, working quickly. Kitty felt her pulse beats beneath the iron fingers of the guard. Resistance was making it worse. She relaxed; first her wrist, then her arm, then she curved her side against him. The guard beside him made what sounded to Kitty like a lewd comment in German before laughing. Adler turned from his task as he finished releasing the first of Luke's arm restraints. Thank God, Kitty thought. It was the secure one.

Kitty saw Adler's frown of displeasure just before Luke's eyes opened, his arm pitched, and splinters of wood flew. The iron bolt arced. Luke used the bolt as ballast as he flung the leather restraint around his tormentor. Kitty crouched. She bit hard at the fingers closing on her wrist. Her keeper gasped, released his hold. She scrambled to Luke's side as he drew the brittle leather around Adler's neck.

The shock in the German's light eyes had already changed to cold fury. "I advise you to kill me, Captain," he said. "You will not get a second chance."

Chapter 22

"Kitty, get my knife," Luke commanded, as he pulled Adler's arm up behind his back. She retrieved it, ignoring the menacing hum. Luke heard a ripping sound, then realized she was taping Adler's mouth. Where had she found the tape, Luke wondered.

Someone moved.

"Stay back!" he warned.

Count the shapes. Five men. Five against two. They weren't the worst of odds. But he didn't yet know if he could stand. He gave thanks for Kitty's shining beauty, which he sensed clearly. Together, they could do this.

He slid off the table, landed. His legs held him. He took a firmer grip on their hostage. It felt like holding a snake just behind its venomous jaws. With the placement of the leather strap, he was in control of Adler's breathing. The man knew it, and Luke surmised that he wished to live another day.

"Let's go," Luke said. Kitty led the way out of the room, turning the lock, then sliding a steel desk in front of the door. She was much stronger than she looked.

"Hey, Luke," she alerted him, "Adler will slow us down. We'd better stash him, you think?"

He wasn't thinking about anything but his own, unsteady limbs, and keeping Adler in his grip without breaking his neck. And she was helping him save face about it. For that alone he loved her. She was right, he couldn't hold the bigger, more powerful man much longer.

"There's a big Cadillac sedan on display in the gangster room," Kitty said, ahead of him again, "How about we put him in the trunk?"

"Good," he agreed.

Kitty led them through the semi-darkness of a place he didn't remember at all. But it seemed she did. In this territory of illusions, the automobile was real. He didn't look into Adler's eyes as he closed the trunk.

Relieved of their burden, Luke slumped against the running board.

Kitty frowned. "Hey. You're not going to fall down on the job are you?"

"Not if I can lean on you."

"Sure. But take this thing." She offered the knife.

Luke replaced it in its leg holster. The Germans kept banging on the door. Adler answered with grunts from the trunk. A wave of nausea intensified in the gut of Luke's body, a body already so far out of balance.

Kitty steadied him against her side. "You'll feel better in the salt air," she half-comforted, half-demanded as she took his arm and some of his weight. She was a small woman, how was she doing this, he wondered. She kept talking. "Hey, I know where there's a phone booth, Luke, right next to a taffy stand on the boardwalk." In her pitched-higher voice, he detected a small breach in her confidence.

When they reached the outside, Luke realized Kitty was right about the air. He took it deep into his lungs. It smelled sweet and salty and like a crankshaft all at once. They passed mammoth black silhouettes against the starlit sky of deep night. The sweetness intensified. At a wooden stall, she released her hold on him. Then she hiked up her nurse's skirt. Higher.

Luke felt his mouth go dry, his face flush. Her gardenia scent filled his being, in the company of a pleasant, intense ache that drove all the others away. Something like a black spider web above white stockings clung to her thigh. Her fingers reached inside the web. Kitty smiled brightly. "There!" she proclaimed, "the secret stash nickel for the phone. Some fancy contraption, huh? Isabelle Marius loaned it to me! What's the matter? Say, you haven't seen it before, have you?"

"N-no," he stammered, at the mercy of his pleasant ache.

"That's good." Her smile went lopsided. She finally dropped the hem of her skirt, allowing him to breathe again. "Hey, you're looking better."

Beyond them, beyond the wood planked walkway, something moved. "Kitty," he breathed out. Her hand slipped into his. He pointed forward, with his chin. Shadows. Yes, she saw them too. Rising up from the wooden walkway on the beach, without sound, like ghosts. Until they menaced the night air with the metallic clicks of their weapons.

They fired. Luke grabbed Kitty's waist, pulled her down, as the glass of the telephone booth's door shattered. The men matched the night. Even their skin was greased black. Luke suppressed the urge to charge them as they circled. Commandos. Up from the water.

Their circle tightened. Anchoring Kitty to his side, Luke held his knife to his own throat. "Stay back," he said.

Still they closed in, but halted when he pressed the knife hard enough to a throbbing vein to draw blood. "I'm not going anywhere without her," he said in a voice strangled, desperate, a voice he didn't recognize as his own.

One of the men ordered a halt. "As you wish, Captain," the smallest of the commandos said quietly in an accented voice. Then he made curt commands in German. Two of the men broke off, heading toward the sounds of the banging, to free Adler and his cohorts. The rest led Kitty and Luke off the boardwalk, down the beach.

As they walked, the ground kept shifting under Luke's feet, making it hard to make his way. Kitty was better at it. He leaned on her. Would they see?

A rubber raft waited against the sand dune. They would have no more chances, once inside the submarine. Luke knew where the vein was, he knew what to do, if time ran out.

Keep me with you, her eyes told him. But he would be of no use to her in the water. He could not swim.

* * *

Kitty burrowed in deeper under Luke's arm. His feet dug into the sand. That's the way, partner, she thought. Hold onto me, as if you are the strong one, when we both know differently. Let them think me afraid and cowering in your protective hold. Just, Holy Mother of God, let those long limbs of yours stay standing. She looked up at that vigilant stare. "I didn't give you back your knife so you could cut your own throat with it!" she whispered.

A smile played on one side of Luke's mouth. His hold on her lightened.

One of their guards snapped out something in German, but Luke silenced him with one of those fierce looks. Kitty wondered if he still had the feather from the Empire State window washer. What would happen to it if they did not survive this? What would happen to his pouch of corn pollen and the Lou Gerhig baseball card, and Isabelle Marius's garter belt? Three men approached: Adler, partnered with two commandos in black, like extra shadows. Behind them were the German agents in civilian clothes. Kitty felt the heat of Adler's rage as he approached them.

Too close, Herr Adler. Luke pressed the knife. His blood flowed in a trickle down his neck. Kitty heard herself sob. She didn't have to playact that sound. Adler stepped back.

"You are a brave man, but inexperienced at the art of war, Captain," he said. "You should have set fire to the gallery before you left. Wax burns so well. You have had two chances and squandered both. No more. You will get in the raft, please."

Luke did not move. Kitty didn't like the way his hands were shaking, the way he eyed the ocean horizon. The knife shifted lower against his neck. Oh God, was he giving up? Look at me, Kitty made her eyes plead. There's still time for us.

There, he understood, she was sure, from that small, cocked-sideways smile. He helped her into the raft.

Kitty stayed planted under Luke's arm as the men rowed over the wave's swells. She looked at his strong jaw, at the way the salt spray was rinsing the blood from the wounds at his cheek and neck. He stared back at the shore. A police siren wailed. That sound made the rowers find new energy.

Kitty felt lighter, less burdened with dread, here on the water. She knew this area off Norton's Point, from the times her brothers used to take her out here before dawn.

Mickey and Joe used her as their drowning victim in their early-morning drills, before their lifeguard duty began. Sometimes a couple of bluefish happened to jump in the boat, too. Kitty saw her brothers' faces again, beaming at her good catch for Mama's frying pan. How dare these people invade her rollers and whitecaps, she thought. How dare they change her memories of this stretch from Norton's Point to Hoffman Island?

The men in the raft signaled their lanterns to the island now. No, it wasn't Hoffman Island, she realized. It was a sleek, black, submarine.

And it was signaling back.

Chapter 23

The hum started back behind Luke's fear. From somewhere deep inside him, Luke also heard the voice of the one who was her husband. We are here. The hum became louder, more insistent. Aeroplanes, coming out of the night sky.

He held Kitty closer against his heart. "You can swim?" he asked.

"Sure."

Of course she can. Did I not tell you? Did I not show you the photos of my mermaid on Coney Island? Her husband reminded him. Luke smiled. "Good."

The Germans rowed faster, with Adler giving curt orders, pointing at Luke. His capture was still important. But not Kitty's. A thin whine, followed by an explosion. Close, sending up a stream on the water. Neither of them was important alive to their own side, maybe.

The Germans now poured all their efforts into getting to the U-boat. All but Adler.

"Women are such bad luck aboard ship, don't you agree, Captain?" he asked in that strange, calm voice as he put a lugar to Kitty's head.

Luke flung his knife. It tore into his enemy's arm. The gun fired.

Luke tackled Kitty's waist. They plunged under the water together.

It was not like the water in arroyos at home. Its salty taste, shocked him as it had off the coast of Spain. Above them, a direct hit. The raft burst apart. Debris, equipment, body parts pounded them deeper under the water. Kitty kept her hold on him.

Yes. Keep kicking those beautiful legs, Luke thought at her.

* * *

Something was pulling them both down. Something heavy, strong. Kitty hiked up her skirt and dug into Isabelle Marius's garter belt for the small knife. She got herself down the length of Luke by way of his sleeve, his vest, his pants leg.

There, at his ankle, clinging: Adler. An explosion from above helped her see the pale determined eyes, the whiteness of his fingers' grip.

Kitty sliced the knife across the whiteness. Air bubbles, instead of a scream. Then billows of red. Then release. She grabbed Luke's sleeve and kicked for the surface.

* * *

Above, the light faded. Luke tried to let go of everything. His vision began.

He was a child again, in the American boarding school. The grim-faced teacher was tying his left hand behind him, so he would learn to use the right. He resisted. That small hand broke away, floated before his eyes, and then headed for the bottom of the ocean floor.

He saw the school's ball field next. There, in front of his team, his tongue was being painted with red pepper juice for shouting a war chant in his own language. The small tongue separated from the mouth of the one-handed child who was himself. It drifted down into the abyss of this Below World.

The brass knuckles of his first lover's brother now gleamed through the green water, pounding into his ribs again. Three of the ribs broke away, through his body, and descended.

From the water's depths appeared the cell in Spain with its pain, its ghosts. Luke tried to close his eyes against the sight of himself there, but could not. He caught the scent of his flesh burning. Those burning fragments of himself joined the rest.

Finally, he saw Adler with the gleaming hypodermic needle. Invading, then eviscerating his thoughts, the only things left that were free, and his own. The broken thoughts transformed themselves into sharp prisms of steel, exploding all of the little that was left of him in an obliterating rage.

There. Done. Scattered across the ocean floor.

His clan brother stood amid the gleaming remains, along with the airman, the one who was Kitty's husband. Both looked whole, glorious. His friend wore his turquoise and silver belt. The airman's white silk scarf was not ripped to pieces with shrapnel and blood, but wrapped around his neck, waving gently.

Both men shook their heads.

"You're a mess," his clan brother said. "Well, reclaim yourself."

"I have no strength," Luke whispered.

"No. It is not strength you lack. It is anger. Your anger is here. Leave it. Now, you have power. Go, my friend."

"Hurry," the airman said, smiling. "Or shall I tell her to let go?"

* * *

He was too still. Kitty checked her grip. It was under his chin and pointing him up, just the way her brothers had taught her during their lifeguard exercises. "Luke," she called as they surmounted another swell. "Breathe."

His chest inflated, his buoyancy increased. "That's the way, ya big lug," she encouraged him. A yellow light shone across the water. She stopped stroking and treaded water. As the rescue row boat approached, she listened to the frantic voices.

"Will you put the damned oars up so I can get a good sighting?"

"Sorry, boss."

"Aw, the G-man is puking again."

"Hey, I see them!"

"What do we do now?"

"Throw a line."

"No, a life preserver. Where's the life preserver? Anyone see the damned life preserver?"

Kitty shook her burden. "Shepherd," she summoned. "The cavalry's here."

Luke groaned.

"Hey!" She shouted, waving toward the rocking vessel. "Forget the life preserver, just give us a hand up."

On shore the different branches of law enforcement, espionage, and homeland defense were in chaos, with Weegee's flash camera popping to make sure that blind was added to their already deaf and dumb. Jack Spenser waded into the surf in his expensive suit and lifted Kitty out of the boat.

She looked over his shoulder. "Where's Luke?" she asked.

"Don't worry, we've got him."

"That's exactly what I'm worried about."

Once in the lifeguard station, Isabelle Marius shooed the hulking men aside. She replaced Kitty's soaked and torn clothes with a bulky lifeguard's robe before sitting her down on a cot.

"These brave soldiers of liberty," she confided as she toweled off Kitty's hair, "they can be warmed by their glory. But for you, Kitty," she motioned Isaiah Morgenstern forward, "a little Napoleon brandy, yes?"

"I bring good news about your sister," the watchmaker added.

Kitty looked up into the man's kind eyes.

"Anya's better?"

"And telling us to bring you home, or she'll cut our hearts out." Isaiah sneered. "Oh, you Croatians, always with the knives! And she wants to see her child minder too."

Isabelle's perfect brow arched. "Ah, then! This is serious, between you and our captain, if he is child-minding your family members, I think."

"Where is he? Where's Luke?"

Isabelle frowned before gesturing to the hulking men on the other side of the lifeguard station house. "They are -- how shall I say it . . .?"

"...Working him over," Isaiah continued for her. "Like he hasn't been worked over enough, I tell them. I already explained what he gave to the Nazis."

Kitty blinked. "You did?"

"Sure. Simple to figure when we got to their hideout back there at the old waxwork parlor. Hasty departures leave many clues." He patted Kitty's cold hands. "And somebody, his sharp accomplice in deception, I think, she did just right, Mrs. Charente. Pressing so hard on the notepad, that was smart."

"No, not smart. I was nervous."

"Good thing. See, we rubbed a pencil over your dents, it make the words clear. Once we read them, I explained your scheme to Mr. Spenser."

"Scheme?"

Mr. Fellig joined the watchmaker. "Spenser's bunch were nervous too you see, after picking up the transmissions on my wireless, about how fast things were moving along here!"

"So. Arthur and I translated. To calm them down, you understand," the watchmaker assured her.

"Mr. Fellig knows Luke's language too?" Kitty asked, astonished.

"No, no, no, my dear girl! He knows ours!" The small man laughed. "Or choice cuts of it, at least!"

Kitty shook her head. "I don't understand."

"Of course you don't, being Catholic or Greek Catholic or Muslim or whatever you Croatians are these days!"

"But..."

"But our captain knew variations that even I did not!" Mr. Fellig huffed. "He gets around, that one!"

"Well, by then the FBI's in on the act," his companion took up the story, "then the straggling-in members of the New York City police department."

The photographer folded his arms as he glanced over to the other end of the lifeguard station and its hulking forms. "Now, Kitty Berry, after our service, what do you think? Morgenstern and me, we're banished!"

"Banished?"

"From our post, standing by the captain."

"'Leave Captain Kayenta to the doctor, now,' they say," Isaiah Morgenstern took up the lament. "Doctors, a broch! What do they know? Our captain needs to see you, that's all. That will bring him out of it! But who is listening to an old unreconstructed veteran of the Lincoln Brigade?"

Isabelle Marius pressed her shoulder. Kitty poured the remains of the jelly glass load of brandy down her throat. She rose, then pushed her way past all the masses of grey, blue and pinstripes except the hovering doctor.

"Get away from him," she demanded.

The doctor looked over her head, to where Jack stood. He nodded. Both men backed off. Kitty gazed down at the cot holding Luke, his lips blue, his eyes, ice hard, staring at the whitewashed ceiling.

"Hey," she called softly. "Look lively, Shepherd. Don't want your own people sticking you with their needles, do you?"

* * *

Kitty's hair was wild, black, swirling around her head unbound. She was wearing a robe that looked like it belonged to a prize fighter. "Joe Berry" was embroidered above her heart. This is how she would look if they slept in the same bed, and she awoke displeased with him. He wanted to tell her that. He wanted to tell her that she was a worse influence on him than those two lugs: one her relation, one his, who had bullied him out of the Below World. But he was too happy to see her, sitting beside him on the bed, close enough to feel her breathing.

"Your ocean tastes terrible," he finally said.

She frowned. "Well, you weren't supposed to drink it!"

"Captain." Isaiah Morgenstern summoned, as he appeared on Kitty's right side, "It's an apology I want out of you, no complaints to this poor girl you forced to do your bidding."

"Forced?" the photographer Weegee countered from her left. "Who forced Kitty Berry? I'll strangle him with my bare hands! I don't care if he's a captain, a major, a general!"

"You want proof?" Isaiah Morgenstern demanded. "You know the proof!"

The watchmaker shoved the notepad before Kitty's other sentinel's eyes. "You saw what meshugine makes her to write with those delicate lady fingers!"

Weegee regarded the page full of code words and translations. His eyebrows rose. "It's bad enough what we heard on the radio from those filthy Germans. This schmendrick made our Kitty write these things?" Suddenly his indignation shifted. A smile halved his face around his ever-present cigar stub. "And the Nazi high command will be hearing it all, maybe?"

"If the slippery eel U-Boat gets across the Atlantic, this is true!" Isaiah conceded, his mood also shifting. Kitty sifted the hair back from Luke's forehead. He closed his eyes, wishing all but her to disappear.

The photographer frowned. "You know, the spelling is terrible."

"She's a shikseh. And our captain's a Red Indian. What do you think, their Yiddish will be perfect?"

Kitty looked up at the hovering forms. "Yiddish?"

Luke enjoyed the astonishment in her voice.

"I was writing Yiddish?"

Behind them, the two men battled on with each other. "It's a good thing for their abominable accents," Isaiah said, "or it would have looked and sounded more German."

"German? Bite your tongue!"

"Arthur Fellig! You've been in America so long you don't know that Yiddish is mostly German?"

"It is?" Luke asked, rising on his elbows.

"Not the American form of Yiddish, that doesn't sound German," Weegee insisted, still in his argument with Morgenstern. "Maybe you been fighting revolutions in Spain too long, hulyen."

"Yiddish?" Kitty asked the squabbling men again.

"I don't think they are talking to us anymore," Luke confided.

They watched Weegee draw himself up in his indignation. "Nevertheless and regardless! Such expressions that a lady should never have to listen to, never mind write! I ask you, where did this boy learn such filth..." Suddenly his gaze shifted to Luke. "Say, what are you smiling at, you degenerate?" he demanded.

"I apologized to her!"

"Never mind! Who taught you those expressions?"

"That's... classified, isn't it, sir?" Luke asked as his superior stepped forward.

Jack Spenser folded his arms. "Oh, no. Don't throw me into this mix." He peered over at Mr. Morgenstern's scribbling-in-the-margins translations, and gave out a low whistle. "Well. Yiddish has got Anglo-Saxon vulgarity beat by a country mile." His brows came together. "And, that one, that's not physically possible, is it?"

Isabelle Marius squeezed herself into the already crowded space around Luke's narrow cot, blankets folded over her arm. She glanced over the paper. "Still, Hitler, Mussolini and Franco should all try it. The war would end tomorrow," she pronounced.

Kitty leaned in closer and grabbed the front of the soft nightshirt they'd put on Luke. "That's what you meant?" she demanded. "That's why I had to trust you? What I wrote was not what they wanted? Not your language at all? We were lying?"

"Please, Madame!" Isabelle defended him. "Regard the words. They are not lies. They are ... inexact translations, I would say. More direct, and well... coarse. And, I imagine, the only Yiddish our dear captain knows. How does he know even this, I ask myself?" The Frenchwoman shifted her gaze around their circle until she found her mark. "Learned from a certain desperate man, in trying times, perhaps in a prison cell in Spain?"

The watchmaker coughed uncomfortably.

Isabelle kissed the small man's balding pate before she began stringing a clothesline around the bed's space. A burly FBI agent patiently handed her the draping blankets.

* * *

Luke liked watching Kitty's dawning understanding as she sat beside him, and among these people who teased each other, much like his own relatives.

Suddenly, she gave those beautiful eyes' attention to him alone. He liked that even more. "You look beat, partner," she whispered.

"We are not beat, Kitty."

Her eyes filled with tears. What had he said wrong? She cradled his head in her arms and began weeping into his hair. Why? He liked it much better when she was fighting with him. But he'd take her this way rather than not at all.

And this way got Isabelle Marius to shove all their extra company out before she drew the last of her privacy curtain around the narrow bed. After a slow wink, Isabelle herself slipped away. Kitty wiped her cheeks with the backs of her hands. Then she growled like a mother bear. That was better.

"Move over," she commanded, "my feet are cold."

The End

Eileen Charbonneau books also publish by BWL Publishing Inc.

I'll Be Seeing You – Navajo Code Talkers - 1

Watch Over Me – Navajo Code Talkers - 2

Seven Aprils – Civil War Brides - 1

Ursula's Inheritance – Civil War Brides - 2

Mercies of the Fallen – Civil War Brides - 3

Death at Little Mound – YA - 1

Missing at Harmony Festival – YA - 2

Stolen at the Wildlife Sanctuary – YA - 3

Eileen Charbonneau is a Rita and Heart of the West award-winning author of novels and screenplays. She's been involved with theater and independent filmmaking projects, and is a storyteller of Irish and Native American tales. Eileen's multi-cultural heritage includes Shoshone relatives who were three members of the Lewis and Clark Expedition. You can reach her through her website:

eileencharbonneau.googlepages.com, her blog: Manituwak.blogspot.com, on facebook as Eileen Charbonneau Author, via Twitter @EileenC1988 or by email: EileenCharbonneau@gmail.com

Eileen Charbonneau's stories explore the perspectives of people often left out of history: women, first peoples and immigrants, marginalized poor.

Eileen has published fiction for adult as well for young readers. She lives in the brave little state of Vermont with her husband Ed. She adores him, her kids and sweet grandchild. Eileen loves reading, watching great movies, exploring her beautiful state, country and world, roots music and dance of all cultures, and Vermont maple creemies. (write to her at eileencharbonneau@gmail.com and she'll tell you what they are!)

Eileen loves to hear from readers. You can find her at:
https://bookswelove.net/charbonneau-eileen/
eileencharbonneau.com
email: eileencharbonneau@gmail.com
twitter: @EileenC1988
Facebook: Eileen Charbonneau Author
Instagram: eileencharbonneau

Blogs: http://manituwak.blogspot.com
https://bwlauthors.blogspot.com

www.ingramcontent.com/pod-product-compliance
Lightning Source LLC
LaVergne TN
LVHW021659060526
838200LV00050B/2430